"You're wasted—bullied by selfish women and changing babies' nappies."

"I like babies." Emma added tartly, "It's kind of you to bother, but there is no need—"

"How old are you, Emma?"

"Almost twenty-six."

Sir Paul smiled. "Twenty-five, going on fifteen! I'm forty—do you find that old?"

"Old? Of course not. You're not yet in your prime. And you don't feel like forty, do you?"

"At the moment I feel thirty at the most!" He smiled at her and she thought what a very nice smile he had—warm and somehow reassuring.

Betty Neels spent her childhood and youth in
Devonshire before training as a nurse and midwife. She
was an army nursing sister during the war, married a
Dutchman, and subsequently lived in Holland for
fourteen years. She lives with her husband in Dorset,
and has a daughter and a grandson. Her hobbies
are reading, animals, old buildings and writing. On
retirement from nursing Betty started to write, incited by
a lady in a library bemoaning the lack of romantic novels.

Mrs. Neels is always delighted to receive fan letters, but
would truly appreciate it if they could be directed to
Harlequin Mills & Boon Ltd., 18-24 Paradise Road,
Richmond, Surrey, TW9 1SR, England.

Books by Betty Neels

HARLEQUIN ROMANCE

The Right Kind of Girl
Betty Neels

Harlequin Books

TORONTO • NEW YORK • LONDON
AMSTERDAM • PARIS • SYDNEY • HAMBURG
STOCKHOLM • ATHENS • TOKYO • MILAN
MADRID • WARSAW • BUDAPEST • AUCKLAND

ISBN 0-373-03467-9

THE RIGHT KIND OF GIRL

First North American Publication 1997.

Copyright © 1995 by Betty Neels.

Printed in U.S.A.

CHAPTER ONE

MRS SMITH-DARCY had woken in a bad temper. She reclined, her abundant proportions supported by a number of pillows, in her bed, not bothering to reply to the quiet 'good morning' uttered by the girl who had entered the room; she was not a lady to waste courtesy on those she considered beneath her. Her late husband had left her rich, having made a fortune in pickled onions, and since she had an excellent opinion of herself she found no need to bother with the feelings of anyone whom she considered inferior. And, of course, a paid companion came into that category.

The paid companion crossed the wide expanse of carpet and stood beside the bed, notebook in hand. She looked out of place in the over-furnished, frilly room; a girl of medium height, with pale brown hair smoothed into a French pleat, she had unremarkable features, but her eyes were large, thickly lashed and of a pleasing hazel. She was dressed in a pleated skirt and a white blouse, with a grey cardigan to match the skirt—sober clothes which failed to conceal her pretty figure and elegant legs.

Mrs Smith-Darcy didn't bother to look at her. 'You can go to the bank and cash a cheque—the servants want their wages. Do call in at the butcher's and tell him that I'm not satisfied with the meat he's sending up to the house. When you get back—and don't be all day over a couple of errands—you can make an appointment with my hairdresser and get the invitations written for my luncheon party. The list's on my desk.'

She added pettishly, 'Well, get on with it, then; there's plenty of work waiting for you when you get back.'

The girl went out of the room without a word, closed the door quietly behind her and went downstairs to the kitchen where Cook had a cup of coffee waiting for her.

'Got your orders, Miss Trent? In a mood, is she?'

'I dare say it's this weather, Cook. I have to go to the shops. Is there anything I can bring back for you?'

'Well, now, love, if you could pop into Mr Coffin's and ask him to send up a couple of pounds of sausages with the meat? They'll do us a treat for our dinner.'

Emma Trent, battling on her bike against an icy February wind straight from Dartmoor and driving rain, reflected that there could be worse jobs, only just at that moment she couldn't think of any. It wasn't just the weather—she had lived in Buckfastleigh all her life and found nothing unusual in that; after all, it was only a mile or so from the heart of the moor with its severe winters.

Bad weather she could dismiss easily enough, but Mrs Smith-Darcy was another matter; a selfish lazy woman, uncaring of anyone's feelings but her own, she was Emma's daily trial, but her wages put the butter on the bread of Emma's mother's small pension so she had to be borne. Jobs weren't all that easy to find in a small rural town, and if she went to Plymouth or even Ashburton it would mean living away from home, whereas now they managed very well, although there was never much money over.

Her errands done, and with the sausages crammed into a pocket, since Mr Coffin had said that he wasn't sure if he could deliver the meat before the afternoon, she cycled back to the large house on the other side of the town where her employer lived, parked her bike by the side-door and went into the kitchen. There she handed over the sausages, hung her sopping raincoat to dry and went along to the little cubby-hole where she spent most of her days—making out cheques for the tradesmen, making appointments, writing notes and keeping the household books. When she wasn't doing that, she arranged the flowers, and answered the door if Alice, the housemaid, was busy or having her day off.

'Never a dull moment,' said Emma to her reflection as she tidied her hair and dried the rain from her face. The buzzer Mrs Smith-Darcy used whenever she demanded Emma's presence was clamouring to be answered, and she picked up her notebook and pencil and went unhurriedly upstairs.

Mrs Smith-Darcy had heaved herself out of bed and was sitting before the dressing-table mirror, doing her face. She didn't look up from the task of applying mascara. 'I have been buzzing you for several minutes,' she observed crossly. 'Where have you been? Really, a great, strong girl like you should have done those few errands in twenty minutes...'

Emma said mildly, 'I'm not a great, strong girl, Mrs Smith-Darcy, and cycling into the wind isn't the quickest way of travelling. Besides, I got wet—'

'Don't make childish excuses. Really, Miss Trent, I sometimes wonder if you are up to this job. Heaven knows, it's easy enough.'

Emma knew better than to answer that. Instead she asked, 'You wanted me to do something for you, Mrs Smith-Darcy?'

'Tell Cook I want my coffee in half an hour. I shall

be out to lunch, and while I'm gone you can fetch Frou-Frou from the vet. I shall need Vickery with the car so I suppose you had better get a taxi—it wouldn't do for Frou-Frou to get wet. You can pay and I'll settle with you later.'

'I haven't brought any money with me.' Emma crossed her fingers behind her back as she spoke, for it was a fib, but on several occasions she had been told to pay for something and that she would be reimbursed later—something which had never happened.

Mrs Smith-Darcy frowned. 'Really, what an incompetent girl you are.' She opened her handbag and found a five-pound note. 'Take this—and I'll expect the correct change.'

'I'll get the driver to write the fare down and sign it,' said Emma quietly, and something in her voice made Mrs Smith-Darcy look at her.

'There's no need for that.'

'It will set your mind at rest,' said Emma sweetly. 'I'll get those invitations written; I can post them on my way home.'

Mrs Smith-Darcy, who liked to have the last word, was for once unable to think of anything to say as Emma left the room.

It was well after five o'clock when Emma got on to her bike and took herself off home—a small, neat house near the abbey where she and her mother had lived since her father had died several years earlier.

He had died suddenly and unexpectedly, and it hadn't been until after his death that Mrs Trent had been told that he had mortgaged the house in order to raise the money to help his younger brother, who had been in financial difficulties, under the impression that he would be repaid within a reasonable time. There hadn't been enough money to pay off the mortgage, so she had sold the house and bought a small terraced house, and, since her brother-in-law had gone abroad without leaving an address, she and Emma now managed on her small pension and Emma's salary. That she herself was underpaid Emma was well aware, but on the other hand her job allowed her to keep an eye on her mother's peptic ulcer...

There was an alley behind the row of houses. She wheeled her bike along its length and into their small back garden, put it in the tumbledown shed outside the kitchen door and went into the house.

The kitchen was small, but its walls were distempered in a cheerful pale yellow and there was room for a small table and two chairs against one wall. She took off her outdoor things, carried them through to the narrow little hall and went into the sitting-room. That was small, too, but it was comfortably furnished, although a bit shabby, and there was a cheerful fire burning in the small grate.

Mrs Trent looked up from her sewing. 'Hello, love. Have you had a tiring day? And so wet and cold too. Supper is in the oven but you'd like a cup of tea first...'

'I'll get it.' Emma dropped a kiss on her mother's cheek and went to make the tea and presently carried it back.

'Something smells heavenly,' she observed. 'What have you been cooking?'

'Casserole and dumplings. Did you get a proper lunch?'

Emma assured her that she had, with fleeting regret for most of the sausages she hadn't been given time to eat; Mrs Smith-Darcy had the nasty habit of demanding that some task must be done at once, never mind how inconvenient. She reflected with pleasure that her em-

ployer was going away for several days, and although
she had been given a list of things to do which would
take at least twice that period it would be like having a
holiday.

She spent the next day packing Mrs Smith-Darcy's
expensive cases with the clothes necessary to make an
impression during her stay at Torquay's finest hotel—a
stay which, she pointed out to Emma, was vital to her
health. This remark reminded her to order the central
heating to be turned down while she was absent. 'And
I expect an accurate statement of the household ex-
penses.'

Life, after Mrs Smith-Darcy had been driven away by
Vickery, the chauffeur, was all of a sudden pleasant.

It was delightful to arrive each morning and get on
with her work without having to waste half an hour listening to her employer's querulous voice raised in crit-
icism about something or other, just as it was delightful
to go home each evening at five o'clock exactly.

Over and above this, Cook, unhampered by her employer's strictures, allowed her creative skills to run free
so that they ate food which was never normally allowed—rich steak and kidney pudding with a drop of
stout in the gravy, roasted potatoes—crisply brown,
toad-in-the-hole, braised celery, cauliflower smothered
in a creamy sauce and all followed by steamed puddings,
sticky with treacle or bathed in custard.

Emma, eating her dinners in the kitchen with Cook
and Alice, the housemaid, savoured every morsel,
dutifully entered the bills in her household ledger and
didn't query any of them; she would have to listen to a
diatribe about the wicked extravagance of her staff from
Mrs Smith-Darcy but it would be worth it, and Cook

had given her a cake to take home, declaring that she had made two when one would have done.

On the last day of Mrs Smith-Darcy's absence from home Emma arrived in good time. There were still one or two tasks to do before that lady returned—the flowers to arrange, the last of the post to sort out and have ready for her inspection, a list of the invitations accepted for the luncheon party...

She almost fell off her bike as she shot through the gates into the short drive to the house. The car was before the door and Vickery was taking the cases out of the boot. He cast his eyes up as she jumped off her bike.

'Took bad,' he said. 'During the night. 'Ad the doctor to see 'er—gave her an injection and told 'er it were a bug going round—gastric something or other. Alice is putting 'er to bed, miss. You'd better go up sharp, like.'

'Oh, Vickery, you must have had to get up very early—it's only just nine o'clock.'

'That I did, miss.' He smiled at her. 'I'll see to yer bike.'

'Thank you, Vickery. I'm sure Cook will have breakfast for you.'

She took off her outdoor things and went upstairs. Mrs Smith-Darcy's door was closed but she could hear her voice raised in annoyance. She couldn't be very ill if she could shout like that, thought Emma, opening the door.

'There you are—never where you're wanted, as usual. I'm ill—very ill. That stupid doctor who came to the hotel told me it was some kind of virus. I don't believe him. I'm obviously suffering from some grave internal disorder. Go and phone Dr Treble and tell him to come at once.'

'He'll be taking surgery,' Emma pointed out reasonably. 'I'll ask him to come as soon as he's finished.' She studied Mrs Smith-Darcy's face. 'Are you in great pain? Did the doctor at Torquay advise you to go to a hospital for emergency treatment?'

'Of course not. If I need anything done I shall go into a private hospital. I am in great pain—agony…' She didn't quite meet Emma's level gaze. 'Do as I tell you; I must be attended to at once.'

She was in bed now, having her pillows arranged just so by the timid Alice. Emma didn't think that she looked in pain; certainly her rather high colour was normal, and if she had been in the agony she described then she wouldn't have been fussing about her pillows and which bed-jacket she would wear. She went downstairs and dialled the surgery.

The receptionist answered. 'Emma—how are you? Your mother's all right? She looked well when I saw her a few days ago.'

'Mother's fine, thanks, Mrs Butts. Mrs Smith-Darcy came back this morning from a few days at Torquay. She wasn't well during the night and the hotel called a doctor who told her it was a bug and that she had better go home—he gave her something—I don't know what. She says she is in great pain and wants Dr Treble to come and see her immediately.'

'The surgery isn't finished—it'll be another half an hour or so, unless she'd like to be brought here in her car.' Mrs Butts chuckled. 'And that's unlikely, isn't it?' She paused. 'Is she really ill, Emma?'

'Her colour is normal; she's very cross…'

'When isn't she very cross? I'll ask Doctor to visit when surgery is over, but, I warn you, if there's anything really urgent he'll have to see to it first.'

Emma went back to Mrs Smith-Darcy and found her sitting up in bed renewing her make-up. 'You're feeling better? Would you like coffee or tea? Or something to eat?'

'Don't be ridiculous, Miss Trent; can you not see how I'm suffering? Is the doctor on his way?'

'He'll come when surgery is finished—about half an hour, Mrs Butts said.'

'Mrs Butts? Do you mean to tell me that you didn't speak to Dr Treble?'

'No, he was busy with a patient.'

'I am a patient,' said Mrs Smith-Darcy in a furious voice.

Emma, as mild as milk and unmoved, said, 'Yes, Mrs Smith-Darcy. I'll be back in a minute; I'm going to open the post while I've the chance.'

There must be easier ways of earning a living, she reflected, going down to the kitchen to ask Cook to make lemonade.

She bore the refreshment upstairs presently, and took it down again as her employer didn't find it sweet enough. When she went back with it she was kept busy closing curtains because the dim light from the February morning was hurting the invalid's eyes, then fetching another blanket to put over her feet, and changing the bed-jacket she had on, which wasn't the right colour...

'Now go and fetch my letters,' said Mrs Smith-Darcy.

Perhaps, thought Emma, nipping smartly downstairs once more, Dr Treble would prescribe something which would soothe the lady and cause her to doze off for long periods. Certainly at the moment Mrs Smith-Darcy had no intention of doing any such thing.

Emma, proffering her post, got the full force of her displeasure.

'Bills,' said Mrs Smith-Darcy. 'Nothing but bills!' And went on that doubtless, while her back was turned, those whom she employed had eaten her out of house and home, and as for an indigent nephew who had had the effrontery to ask her for a small loan... 'Anyone would think that I was made of money,' she said angrily—which was, in fact, not far wrong.

The richer you are, the meaner you get, reflected Emma, retrieving envelopes and bills scattered over the bed and on the floor.

She was on her knees with her back to the door when it was opened and Alice said, 'The doctor, ma'am,' and something in her voice made Emma turn around. It wasn't Dr Treble but a complete stranger who, from her lowly position, looked enormous.

Indeed, he was a big man; not only very tall but built to match his height, he was also possessed of a handsome face with a high-bridged nose and a firm mouth. Pepper and salt hair, she had time to notice, and on the wrong side of thirty. She was aware of his barely concealed look of amusement as she got to her feet.

'Get up, girl,' said Mrs Smith-Darcy and then added, 'I sent for Dr Treble.' She took a second look at him and altered her tone. 'I don't know you, do I?'

He crossed the room to the bed. 'Dr Wyatt. I have taken over from Dr Treble for a short period. What can I do for you, Mrs Smith-Darcy? I received a message that it was urgent.'

'Oh, Doctor, I have had a shocking experience—' She broke off for a moment. 'Miss Trent, get the doctor a chair.'

But before Emma could move he had picked up a spindly affair and sat on it, seemingly unaware of the alarming creaks; at the same time he had glanced at her again with the ghost of a smile. Nice, thought Emma, making herself as inconspicuous as possible. I hope that he will see through her. At least she won't be able to bully him like she does Dr Treble.

Her hopes were justified. Mrs Smith-Darcy, prepared to discuss her symptoms at some length, found herself answering his questions with no chance of embellishment, although she did her best.

'You dined last evening?' he wanted to know. 'What exactly did you eat and drink?'

'The hotel is noted for its excellent food,' she gushed. 'It's expensive, of course, but one has to pay for the best, does one not?' She waited for him to make some comment and then, when he didn't, added pettishly, 'Well, a drink before I dined, of course, and some of the delightful canapés they serve. I have a small appetite but I managed a little caviare. Then, let me see, a morsel of sole with a mushroom sauce—cooked in cream, of course—and then a simply delicious pheasant with an excellent selection of vegetables.'

'And?' asked Dr Wyatt, his voice as bland as his face.

'Oh, dessert—meringue with a chocolate sauce laced with curaçao—a small portion, I might add.' She laughed. 'A delicious meal—'

'And the reason for your gastric upset. There is nothing seriously wrong, Mrs Smith-Darcy, and it can be easily cured by taking some tablets which you can obtain from the chemist and then keeping to a much plainer diet in future. I'm sure that your daughter—'

'My paid companion,' snapped Mrs Smith-Darcy. 'I am a lonely widow, Doctor, and able to get about very little.'

'I suggest that you take regular exercise each day—a brisk walk, perhaps.'

Mrs Smith-Darcy shuddered. 'I feel that you don't understand my delicate constitution, Doctor; I hope that I shan't need to call you again.'

'I think it unlikely; I can assure you that there is nothing wrong with you, Mrs Smith-Darcy. You will feel better if you get up and dress.'

He bade her goodbye with cool courtesy. 'I will give your companion some instructions and write a prescription for some tablets.'

Emma opened the door for him, but he took the handle from her and ushered her through before closing it gently behind him.

'Is there somewhere we might go?'

'Yes—yes, of course.' She led the way downstairs and into her office.

He looked around him. 'This is where you work at being a companion?'

'Yes. Well, I do the accounts and bills and write the letters here. Most of the time I'm with Mrs Smith-Darcy.'

'But you don't live here?' He had a pleasant, deep voice, quite quiet and soothing, and she answered his questions readily because he sounded so casual.

'No, I live in Buckfastleigh with my mother.'

'A pleasant little town. I prefer the other end, though, nearer the abbey.'

'Oh, so do I; that's where we are...' She stopped there; he wouldn't want to know anything about her— they were strangers, not likely to see each other again. 'Is there anything special I should learn about Mrs Smith-Darcy?'

'No, she is perfectly healthy although very overweight. Next time she overeats try to persuade her to take one of these tablets instead of calling the doctor.'

He was writing out a prescription and paused to look at her. 'You're wasted here, you know.'

She blushed. 'I've not had any training—at least, only shorthand and typing and a little bookkeeping—and there aren't many jobs here.'

'You don't wish to leave home?'

'No. I can't do that. Is Dr Treble ill?'

'Yes, he's in hospital. He has had a heart attack and most likely will retire.'

She gave him a thoughtful look. 'I'm very sorry. You don't want me to tell Mrs Smith-Darcy?'

'No. In a little while the practice will be taken over by another doctor.'

'You?'

He smiled. 'No, no. I'm merely filling in until things have been settled.'

He gave her the prescription and closed his bag. The hand he offered was large and very firm and she wanted to keep her hand in his. He was, she reflected, a very nice man—dependable; he would make a splendid friend. It was such an absurd idea that she smiled and he decided that her smile was enchanting.

She went to the door with him and saw the steel-grey Rolls Royce parked in the drive. 'Is that yours?' she asked.

'Yes.' He sounded amused and she begged his pardon and went pink again and stood, rather prim, in the open door until he got in and drove away.

She turned, and went in and up to the bedroom to find Mrs Smith-Darcy decidedly peevish. 'Really, I don't know what is coming to the medical profession,' she began, the moment Emma opened the door. 'Nothing wrong with me, indeed; I never heard such nonsense.

I'm thoroughly upset. Go down and get my coffee and some of those wine biscuits.'

'I have a prescription for you, Mrs Smith-Darcy,' said Emma. 'I'll fetch it while you're getting dressed, shall I?'

'I have no intention of dressing. You can go to the chemist while I'm having my coffee—and don't hang around. There's plenty for you to do here.'

When she got back Mrs Smith-Darcy asked, 'What has happened to Dr Treble? I hope that that man is replacing him for a very short time; I have no wish to see him again.'

To which remark Emma prudently made no answer. Presently she went off to the kitchen to tell Cook that her mistress fancied asparagus soup made with single cream and a touch of parsley, and two lamb cutlets with creamed potatoes and braised celery in a cheese sauce. So much for the new doctor's advice, reflected Emma, ordered down to the cellar to fetch a bottle of Bollinger to tempt the invalid's appetite.

That evening, sitting at supper with her mother, Emma told her of the new doctor. 'He was nice. I expect if you were really ill he would take the greatest care of you.'

'Elderly?' asked Mrs Trent artlessly.

'Something between thirty and thirty-five, I suppose. Pepper and salt hair...'

A not very satisfactory answer from her mother's point of view.

February, tired of being winter, became spring for a couple of days, and Emma, speeding to and fro from Mrs Smith-Darcy's house, had her head full of plans—a day out with her mother on the following Sunday. She could rent a car from Dobbs's garage and drive her mother to

Widecombe in the Moor and then on to Bovey Tracey;
they could have lunch there and then go on back home
through Ilsington—no main roads, just a quiet jaunt
around the country they both loved.

She had been saving for a tweed coat and skirt, but
she told herself that since she seldom went anywhere,
other than a rare visit to Exeter or Plymouth, they could
wait until autumn. She and her mother both needed a
day out...

The weather was kind; Sunday was bright and clear,
even if cold. Emma got up early, fed Queenie, their elderly cat, took tea to her mother and got the breakfast
and, while Mrs Trent cleared it away, went along to the
garage and fetched the car.

Mr Dobbs had known her father and was always willing to rent her a car, letting her have it at a reduced price
since it was usually the smallest and shabbiest in his
garage, though in good order, as he was always prompt
to tell her. Today she was to have an elderly Fiat, bright
red and with all the basic comforts, but, she was assured,
running well. Emma, casting her eye over it, had a mo-
mentary vision of a sleek Rolls Royce...

They set off in the still, early morning and, since they
had the day before them, Emma drove to Ashburton and
presently took the narrow moor road to Widecombe,
where they stopped for coffee before driving on to
Bovey Tracey. It was too early for lunch, so they drove
on then to Lustleigh, an ancient village deep in the moorland, the hills around it dotted with granite boulders. But
although the houses and cottages were built of granite
there was nothing forbidding about them—they were
charming even on a chilly winter's day, the thatched
roofs gleaming with the last of the previous night's frost,
smoke eddying gently from their chimney-pots.

Scattered around the village were several substantial houses, tucked cosily between the hills. They were all old—as old as the village—and several of them were prosperous farms while others stood in sheltered grounds.

'I wouldn't mind living here,' said Emma as they passed one particularly handsome house, standing well back from the narrow road, the hills at its back, sheltered by carefully planted trees. 'Shall we go as far as Lustleigh Cleave and take a look at the river?'

After that it was time to find somewhere for lunch. Most of the cafés and restaurants in the little town were closed, since the tourist season was still several months away, but they found a pub where they were served roast beef with all the trimmings and home-made mince tarts to follow.

Watching her mother's pleasure at the simple, well-cooked meal, Emma promised herself that they would do a similar trip before the winter ended, while the villages were quiet and the roads almost empty.

It was still fine weather but the afternoon was already fading, and she had promised to return the car by seven o'clock at the latest. They decided to drive straight home and have tea when they got in, and since it was still a clear afternoon they decided to take a minor road through Ilsington. Emma had turned off the main road on to the small country lane when her mother slumped in her seat without uttering a sound. Emma stopped the car and turned to look at her unconscious parent.

She said, 'Mother—Mother, whatever is the matter...?' And then she pulled herself together—bleating her name wasn't going to help. She undid her safety-belt, took her mother's pulse and called her name again, but Mrs Trent lolled in her seat, her eyes closed. At least

Emma could feel her pulse, and her breathing seemed normal.

Emma looked around her. The lane was narrow; she would never be able to turn the car and there was little point in driving on as Ilsington was a small village—too small for a doctor. She pulled a rug from the back seat and wrapped it round her mother and was full of thankful relief when Mrs Trent opened her eyes, but the relief was short-lived. Mrs Trent gave a groan. 'Emma, it's such a pain, I don't think I can bear it...'

There was only one thing to do—to reverse the car back down the lane, return to the main road and race back to Bovey Tracey.

'It's all right, Mother,' said Emma. 'It's not far to Bovey... There's the cottage hospital there; they'll help you.'

She began to reverse, going painfully slowly since the lane curved between high hedges, and it was a good thing she did, for the oncoming car behind her braked smoothly inches from her boot. She got out so fast that she almost tumbled over; here was help! She had no eyes for the other car but rushed to poke her worried face through the window that its driver had just opened.

'It's you!' she exclaimed. 'Oh, you can help. Only, please come quickly.' Dr. Wyatt didn't utter a word but he was beside her before she could draw another breath. 'Mother—it's Mother; she's collapsed and she's in terrible pain. I couldn't turn the car and this lane goes to Ilsington, and it's on the moor miles from anywhere...'

He put a large, steadying hand on her arm. 'Shall I take a look?'

Mrs Trent was a nasty pasty colour and her hand, when he took it, felt cold and clammy. Emma, half-in, half-out of the car on her side, said, 'Mother's got an ulcer—a peptic ulcer; she takes alkaline medicine and small meals and extra milk.'

He was bending over Mrs Trent. 'Will you undo her coat and anything else in the way? I must take a quick look. I'll fetch my bag.'

He straightened up presently. 'Your mother needs to be treated without delay. I'll put her into my car and drive to Exeter. You follow as soon as you can.'

'Yes.' She cast him a bewildered look.

'Problems?' he asked.

'I rented the car from Dobbs's garage; it has to be back by seven o'clock.'

'I'm going to give your mother an injection to take away the pain. Go to my car; there's a phone between the front seats. Phone this Dobbs, tell him what has happened and say that you'll bring the car back as soon as possible.' He turned his back on Mrs Trent, looming over Emma so that she had to crane her neck to see his face. 'I am sure that your mother has a perforated ulcer, which means surgery as soon as possible.'

She stared up at him, pale with shock, unable to think of anything to say. She nodded once and ran back to his car, and by the time she had made her call she had seen him lift her mother gently and carry her to the car. They made her comfortable on the back seat and Emma was thankful to see that her mother appeared to be dozing. 'She'll be all right? You'll hurry, won't you? I'll drive on until I can turn and then I'll come to the hospital— which one?'

'The Royal Devon and Exeter—you know where it is?' He got into his car and began to reverse down the lane. If the circumstances hadn't been so dire, she would have stayed to admire the way he did it—with the same ease as if he were going forwards.

She got into her car, then, and drove on for a mile or more before she came to a rough track leading on to the moor, where she reversed and drove back the way she had come. She was shaking now, in a panic that her mother was in danger of her life and she wouldn't reach the hospital in time, but she forced herself to drive carefully. Once she reached the main road and turned on to the carriageway, it was only thirteen miles to Exeter...

She forced herself to park the car neatly in the hospital forecourt and walk, not run, in through the casualty entrance. There, thank heaven, they knew who she was and why she had come. Sister, a cosy body with a soft Devon voice, came to meet her.

'Miss Trent? Your mother in is Theatre; the professor is operating at the moment. You come and sit down in the waiting-room and a nurse will bring you a cup of tea—you look as though you could do with it. Your mother is in very good hands, and as soon as she is back in her bed you shall go and see her. In a few minutes I should like some details, but you have your tea first.'

Emma nodded; if she had spoken she would have burst into tears; her small world seemed to be tumbling around her ears. She drank her tea, holding the cup in both hands since she was still shaking, and presently, when Sister came back, she gave her the details she needed in a wooden little voice. 'Will it be much longer?' she asked.

Sister glanced at the clock. 'Not long now. I'm sure you'll be told the moment the operation is finished. Will you go back to Buckfastleigh this evening?'

'Could I stay here? I could sit here, couldn't I? I wouldn't get in anyone's way.'

'If you are to stay we'll do better than that, my dear. Do you want to telephone anyone?'

Emma shook her head. 'There's only Mother and me.' She tried to smile and gave a great sniff. 'So sorry, it's all happened so suddenly.'

'You have a nice cry if you want to. I must go and see what's happening. There's been a street-fight and we'll be busy…'

Emma sat still and didn't cry—when she saw her mother she must look cheerful—so that when somebody came at last she turned a rigidly controlled face to hear the news.

Dr Wyatt was crossing the room to her. 'Your mother is going to be all right, Emma.' And then he held her in his arms as she burst into tears.

CHAPTER TWO

EMMA didn't cry for long but hiccuped, sniffed, sobbed a bit and drew away from him to blow her nose on the handkerchief he offered her.

'You're sure? Was it a big operation? Were you in the theatre?'

'Well, yes. It was quite a major operation but successful, I'm glad to say. You may see your mother; she will be semi-conscious but she'll know that you are there. She's in Intensive Care just for tonight. Tomorrow she will go to a ward—' He broke off as Sister joined them.

'They're wanting you on Male Surgical, sir—urgently.'

He nodded at Emma and went away.

'Mother's going to get well,' said Emma. She heaved a great sigh. 'What would I have done if Dr Wyatt hadn't been driving down the lane when Mother was taken ill? He works here as well as taking over the practice at home?'

Sister looked surprised and then smiled. 'Indeed he works here; he's our Senior Consultant Surgeon, although he's supposed to be taking a sabbatical, but I hear he's helping out Dr Treble for a week or two.'

'So he's a surgeon, not a GP?'

Sister smiled again. 'Sir Paul Wyatt is a professor of surgery, and much in demand for consultations, lecture-tours and seminars. You were indeed fortunate that he happened to be there when you needed help so urgently.'

'Would Mother have died, Sister?'

'Yes, love.'

'He saved her life...' She would, reflected Emma, do anything—anything at all—to repay him. Sooner or later there would be a chance. Perhaps not for years, but she wouldn't forget.

She was taken to see her mother then, who was lying in a tangle of tubes, surrounded by monitoring screens but blessedly awake. Emma bent to kiss her white face, her own face almost as white. 'Darling, everything's fine; you're going to be all right. I'll be here and come and see you in the morning after you've had a good sleep.'

Her mother frowned. 'Queenie,' she muttered.

'I'll phone Mr Dobbs and ask him to put some food outside the cat-flap.'

'Yes, do that, Emma.' Mrs Trent closed her eyes.

Emma turned at the touch on her arm. 'You're going to stay for the night?' A pretty, young nurse smiled at her. 'There's a rest-room on the ground floor; we'll call you if there's any need but I think your mother will sleep until the morning. You can see her before you go home then.'

Emma nodded. 'Is there a phone?'

'Yes, just by the rest-room, and there's a canteen down the corridor where you can get tea and sandwiches.'

'You're very kind.' Emma took a last look at her mother and went to the rest-room. There was no one else there and there were comfortable chairs and a table with magazines on it. As she hesitated at the door the sister from Casualty joined her.

'There's a washroom just across the passage. Try and sleep a little, won't you?'

When she had hurried away Emma picked up the phone. Mr Dobbs was sympathetic and very helpful—of course he'd see to Queenie, and Emma wasn't to worry about the car. 'Come back when you feel you can, love,' he told her. 'And you'd better keep the car for a day or two so's you can see your ma as often as possible.'

Mrs Smith-Darcy was an entirely different kettle of fish. 'My luncheon party,' she exclaimed. 'You will have to come back tomorrow morning and see to it; I am not strong enough to cope with it—you know how delicate I am. It is most inconsiderate of you...'

'My mother,' said Emma, between her teeth, 'in case you didn't hear what I have told you, is dangerously ill. I shall stay here with her as long as necessary. And you are not in the least delicate, Mrs Smith-Darcy, only spoilt and lazy and very selfish!'

She hung up, her ear shattered by Mrs Smith-Darcy's furious bellow. Well, she had burnt her boats, cooked her goose and would probably be had up for libel—or was it slander? She didn't care. She had given voice to sentiments she had choked back for more than a year and she didn't care.

She felt better after her outburst, even though she was now out of work. She drank some tea and ate sandwiches from the canteen, resisted a wish to go in search of someone and ask about her mother, washed her face and combed her hair, plaited it and settled in the easiest of the chairs. Underneath her calm front panic and fright bubbled away.

Her mother might have a relapse; she had looked so dreadfully ill. She would need to be looked after for weeks, which was something Emma would do with loving care, but they would be horribly short of money. There was no one around, so she was able to shed a few tears; she was lonely and scared and tired. She mumbled her prayers and fell asleep before she had finished them.

Sir Paul Wyatt, coming to check his patient's condition at two o'clock in the morning and satisfied with it, took himself down to the rest-room. If Emma was awake he would be able to reassure her…

She was curled up in the chair, her knees drawn up under her chin, the half of her face he could see tear-stained, her thick rope of hair hanging over one shoulder. She looked very young and entirely without glamour, and he knew that when she woke in the morning she would have a job uncoiling herself from the tight ball into which she had wound herself.

He went and fetched a blanket from Casualty and laid it carefully over her; she was going to be stiff in the morning—there was no need for her to be cold as well. He put his hand lightly on her hair, touched by the sight of her, and then smiled and frowned at the sentimental gesture and went away again.

Emma woke early, roused by a burst of activity in Casualty, and just as Sir Paul Wyatt had foreseen, discovered that she was stiff and cramped. She got up awkwardly, folding the blanket neatly, and wondered who had been kind during the night. Then she went to wash her face and comb her hair.

Even with powder and lipstick she still looked a mess—not that it mattered, since there was no one to see her. She rubbed her cheeks to get some colour into them and practised a smile in the looking-glass so that her mother would see how cheerful and unworried she was. She would have to drive back to Buckfastleigh after she had visited her and somehow she would come each day to see her, although at the moment she wasn't sure how. Of one thing she was sure—Mrs Smith-Darcy would have dismissed her out-of-hand, so she would have her days free.

She drank tea and polished off some toast in the canteen, then went to find someone who would tell her when she might see her mother. She didn't have far to go— coming towards her along the passage was Sir Paul Wyatt, immaculate in clerical grey and spotless linen, freshly shaved, his shoes brilliantly polished. She wished him a good morning and, without waiting for him to answer, asked, 'Mother—is she all right? May I see her?'

'She had a good night, and of course you may see her.'

He stood looking at her, and the relief at his words was somewhat mitigated by knowing that her scruffy appearance seemed even more scruffy in contrast to his elegance. She rushed into speech to cover her awkwardness. 'They have been very kind to me here...'

He nodded with faint impatience—of course, he was a busy man and hadn't any time to waste. 'I'll go to Mother now,' she told him. 'I'm truly grateful to you for saving Mother. She's going to be quite well again, isn't she?'

'Yes, but you must allow time for her to regain her strength. I'll take you up to the ward on my way.'

She went with him silently, through corridors and then in a lift and finally through swing-doors where he beckoned a nurse, spoke briefly, then turned on his heel with a quick nod, leaving her to follow the nurse into the ward beyond.

Her mother wasn't in the ward but in a small room

beyond, sitting up in bed. She looked pale and tired but she was smiling, and Emma had to fight her strong wish to burst into tears at the sight of her. She smiled instead. 'Mother, dear, you look so much better. How do you feel? And how nice that you're in a room by yourself…'

She bent and kissed her parent. 'I've just seen Sir Paul Wyatt and he says everything is most satisfactory.' She pulled up a chair and sat by the bed, taking her mother's hand in hers. 'What a coincidence that he should be here. Sister told me that he's a professor of surgery.'

Her mother smiled. 'Yes, love, and I'm fine. I really am. You're to go home now and not worry.'

'Yes, Mother. I'll phone this evening and I'll be back tomorrow. Do you want me to bring anything? I'll pack nighties and slippers and so on and bring them with me.'

Her mother closed her eyes. 'Yes, you know what to bring…'

Emma bent to kiss her again. 'I'm going now; you're tired. Have a nap, darling.'

It was still early; patients were being washed and tended before the breakfast trolley arrived. Emma was too early for the ward sister but the night staff nurse assured her that she would be told if anything unforeseen occurred. 'But your mother is most satisfactory, Miss Trent. The professor's been to see her already; he came in the night too. He's away for most of the day but his registrar is a splendid man. Ring this evening, if you like. You'll be coming tomorrow?'

Emma nodded. 'Can I come any time?'

'Afternoon or evening is best.'

Emma went down to the car and drove herself back to Buckfastleigh. As she went she planned her day. She would have to go and see Mrs Smith-Darcy and explain that she wouldn't be able to work for her any more. That lady was going to be angry and she supposed that she would have to apologise... She was owed a week's wages too, and she would need it.

Perhaps Mr Dobbs would let her hire the car each day just for the drive to and from the hospital; it would cost more than bus fares but it would be much quicker. She would have to go to the bank too; there wasn't much money there but she was prepared to spend the lot if necessary. It was too early to think about anything but the immediate future.

She took the car back to the garage and was warmed by Mr Dobbs's sympathy and his assurance that if she needed it urgently she had only to say so. 'And no hurry to pay the bill,' he promised her.

She went home then, and fed an anxious Queenie before making coffee. She was hungry, but it was past nine o'clock by now and Mrs Smith-Darcy would have to be faced before anything else. She had a shower, changed into her usual blouse, skirt and cardigan, did her face, brushed her hair into its usual smoothness and got on to her bike.

Alice opened the door to her. 'Oh, miss, whatever's happened? The mistress is in a fine state. Cook says come and have a cup of tea before you go up to her room; you'll need all your strength.'

'How kind of Cook,' said Emma. 'I think I'd rather have it afterwards, if I may.' She ran upstairs and tapped on Mrs Smith-Darcy's door and went in.

Mrs Smith-Darcy wasted no time in expressing her opinion of Emma; she repeated it several times before she ran out of breath, which enabled Emma to say, 'I'm sorry if I was rude to you on the phone, Mrs Smith-Darcy, but you didn't seem to understand that my mother was seriously ill—still is. I shall have to go to the hospital each day until she is well enough to come home, when I shall have to look after her until she is quite recovered—and that will take a considerable time.'

'My luncheon party,' gabbled Mrs Smith-Darcy. 'You wicked girl, leaving me like this. I'm incapable...'

Emma's efforts to behave well melted away. 'Yes, you are incapable,' she agreed. 'You're incapable of sympathy or human kindness. I suggest that you get up, Mrs Smith-Darcy, and see to your luncheon party yourself. I apologised to you just now—that was a mistake. You're everything I said and a lot more beside.'

She went out of the room and closed the door gently behind here. Then she opened it again. 'Will you be good enough to send my wages to my home?' She closed the door again on Mrs Smith-Darcy's enraged gasp.

She was shaking so much that her teeth rattled against the mug of tea Cook offered her.

'Now, don't you mind what she says,' said Cook. 'Nasty old lady she is, too. You go on home and have a good sleep, for you're fair worn out. I've put up a pasty and one or two snacks, like; you take them home and if you've no time to cook you just slip round here to the back door—there's always a morsel of something in the fridge.'

The dear soul's kindness was enough to make Emma weep; she sniffed instead, gave Cook a hug and then got on her bike and cycled home, where she did exactly what that lady had told her to do—undressed like lightning and got into bed. She was asleep within minutes.

She woke suddenly to the sound of the door-knocker being thumped.

'Mother,' said Emma, and scrambled out of bed, her heart thumping as loudly as the knocker. Not bothering with slippers, she tugged her dressing-gown on as she flew downstairs. It was already dusk; she had slept for hours—too long—she should have phoned the hospital. She turned the key in the lock and flung the door open.

Professor Sir Paul Wyatt was on the doorstep. He took the door from her and came in and shut it behind him. 'It is most unwise to open your door without putting up the chain or making sure that you know who it is.'

She eyed him through a tangle of hair. 'How can I know if I don't look first, and there isn't a chain?' Her half-awake brain remembered then.

'Mother—what's happened? Why are you here?' She caught at his sleeve. 'She's worse...'

His firm hand covered hers. 'Your mother is doing splendidly; she's an excellent patient. I'm sorry, I should have realised... You were asleep.'

She curled her cold toes on the hall carpet and nodded. 'I didn't mean to sleep for so long; it's getting dark.' She looked up at him. 'Why are you here, then?'

'I'm on my way home, but it has occurred to me that I shall be taking morning surgery here for the next week or two. I'll drive you up to Exeter after my morning visits and bring you back in time for evening surgery here.'

'Oh, would you? Would you really do that? How very kind of you, but won't it be putting you out? Sister said that you were taking a sabbatical, and that means you're on holiday, doesn't it?'

'Hardly a holiday, and I'm free to go in and out as I wish.'

'But you live in Exeter?'

'No, but not far from it; I shall not be in the least inconvenienced.'

She looked at him uncertainly, for he sounded casual

and a little annoyed, but before she could speak he went on briskly, 'You'd better go and put some clothes on. Have you food in the house?'

'Yes, thank you. Cook gave me a pasty.' She was suddenly hungry at the thought of it. 'It was kind of you to come. I expect you want to go home—your days are long...'

He smiled. 'I'll make a pot of tea while you dress, and while we are drinking it I can explain exactly what I've done for your mother.'

She flew upstairs and flung on her clothes, washed her face and tied back her hair. Never mind how she looked—he wouldn't notice and he must be wanting to go home, wherever that was.

She perceived that he was a handy man in the kitchen—the tea was made, Queenie had been fed, and he had found a tin of biscuits.

'No milk, I'm afraid,' he said, not looking up from pouring the tea into two mugs. And then, very much to her surprise he asked, 'Have you sufficient money?'

'Yes—yes, thank you, and Mrs Smith-Darcy owes me a week's wages.' Probably in the circumstances she wouldn't get them, but he didn't need to know that.

He nodded, handed her a mug and said, 'Now, as to your mother...'

He explained simply in dry-as-dust words which were neither threatening nor casual. 'Your mother will stay in hospital for a week—ten days, perhaps—then I propose to send her to a convalescent home—there is a good one at Moretonhampstead, not too far from here—just for a few weeks. When she returns home she should be more or less able to resume her normal way of living, although she will have to keep to some kind of a diet. Time enough for that, however. Will you stay here alone?' He glanced at her. 'Perhaps you have family or a friend who would come...?'

'No family—at least, father had some cousins some-where in London but they don't—that is, since he died we haven't heard from them. I've friends all over Buckfastleigh, though. If I asked one of them I know they'd come and stay but there's no need. I'm not nervous; besides, I'll try and find some temporary work until Mother comes home.'

'Mrs Smith-Darcy has given you the sack?'

'I'm sure of it. I was very rude to her this morning.' Anxious not to invite his pity, she added, 'There's always part-time work here—the abbey shop or the otter sanctuary.' True enough during the season—some months away!

He put down his mug. 'Good. I'll call for you some time after twelve o'clock tomorrow morning.' His good-bye was brief.

Left alone, she put the pasty to warm in the oven, washed the mugs and laid out a tray. The house was cold—there had never been enough money for central heating, and it was too late to make a fire in the sitting-room. She ate her supper, had a shower and went to bed, reassured by her visitor's calm manner and his certainty that her mother was going to be all right. He was nice, she thought sleepily, and not a bit pompous. She slept on the thought.

It was raining hard when she woke and there was a vicious wind driving off the moor. She had breakfast and hurried round to Dobbs's garage to use his phone. Her mother had had a good night, she was told, and was looking forward to seeing her later—reassuring news, which sent her back to give the good news to Queenie and then do the housework while she planned all the things she would do before her mother came home.

She had a sandwich and a cup of coffee well before twelve o'clock, anxious not to keep the professor waiting, so that when he arrived a few minutes before that hour she was in her coat, the house secure, Queenie settled in her basket and the bag she had packed for her mother ready in the hall.

He wished her a friendly good morning, remarked upon the bad weather and swept her into the car and drove away without wasting a moment. Conversation, she soon discovered, wasn't going to flourish in the face of his monosyllabic replies to her attempts to make small talk. She decided that he was tired or mulling over his patients and contented herself with watching the bleak landscape around them.

At the hospital he said, 'Will half-past four suit you? Be at the main entrance, will you?' He added kindly, 'I'm sure you'll be pleased with your mother's progress.' He got out of the car and opened her door, waited while she went in and then, contrary to her surmise, drove out of the forecourt and out of the city. Emma, unaware of this, expecting him to be about his own business in the hospital, made her way to her mother's room and forgot him at once.

Her mother was indeed better—pale still, and hung around with various tubes, but her hair had been nicely brushed and when Emma had helped her into her pink bed-jacket she looked very nearly her old self.

'It's a miracle, isn't it?' said Emma, gently embracing her parent. 'I mean, it's only forty-eight or so hours and here you are sitting up in bed.'

Mrs Trent, nicely sedated still, agreed drowsily. 'You brought my knitting? Thank you, dear. Is Queenie all right? And how are you managing to come? It can't be easy—don't come every day; it's such a long way…'

'Professor Wyatt is standing in for Dr Treble, so he brings me here after morning surgery and takes me back in time for his evening surgery.'

'That's nice.' Mrs Trent gave Emma's hand a little squeeze. 'So I'll see you each day; I'm so glad.' She closed her eyes and dropped off and Emma sat holding her hand, making plans.

A job—that was the most important thing to consider; a job she would be able to give up when her mother returned home. She might not be trained for anything much but she could type well enough and she could do simple accounts and housekeep adequately enough; there was sure to be something…

Her mother woke presently and she talked cheerfully about everyday things, not mentioning Mrs Smith-Darcy and, indeed, she didn't intend to do so unless her mother asked.

A nurse came and Emma, watching her skilful handling of tubes and the saline drip, so wished that she could be cool and calm and efficient and—an added bonus—pretty. Probably she worked for the professor—saw him every day, was able to understand him when he gave his orders in strange surgical terms, and received his thanks. He seemed to Emma to be a man of effortless good manners.

Her mother dozed again and didn't rouse as the tea-trolley was wheeled in, which was a good thing since a cup of tea was out of the question, but Emma was given one, with two Petit Beurre biscuits, and since her hurried lunch seemed a long time ago she was grateful.

Her mother was soon awake again, content to lie quietly, not talking much and finally with an eye on the clock, Emma kissed her goodbye. 'I'll be here tomorrow,' she promised, and went down to the main entrance.

She had just reached it when the Rolls came soundlessly to a halt beside her. The professor got out and opened her door, got back in and drove away with nothing more than a murmured greeting, but presently he said, 'Your mother looks better, does she not?'

'Oh, yes. She slept for most of the afternoon but she looks much better than I expected.'

'Of course, she's being sedated, and will be for the next forty-eight hours. After that she will be free of pain and taking an interest in life again. She's had a tiring time…'

It was still raining—a cold rain driven by an icy wind—and the moor looked bleak and forbidding in the early dusk. Emma, who had lived close to it all her life, was untroubled by that; she wondered if the professor felt the same. He had said that he lived near Exeter. She wondered exactly where; perhaps, after a few days of going to and fro, he would be more forthcoming. Certainly he was a very silent man.

The thought struck her that he might find her boring, but on the following day, when she ventured a few remarks of a commonplace nature, he had little to say in reply, although he sounded friendly enough. She decided that silence, unless he began a conversation, was the best policy, so that by the end of a week she was no nearer knowing anything about him than when they had first met. She liked him—she liked him very much—but she had the good sense to know that they inhabited different worlds. He had no wish to get to know her—merely to offer a helping hand, just as he would have done with anyone else in similar circumstances.

Her mother was making good progress and Emma scanned the local paper over the weekend, and checked the advertisements outside the newsagents in the hope of finding a job.

Mrs Smith-Darcy had, surprisingly, sent Alice with her wages, and Emma had made a pot of coffee and listened to Alice's outpourings on life with that lady. 'Mad as fire, she was,' Alice had said, with relish. 'You should 'ave 'eard 'er, Miss Trent. And that lunch party— that was a lark and no mistake—'er whingeing away about servants and such like. I didn't 'ear no kind words about you and your poor ma, though. Mean old cat.' She had grinned. 'Can't get another companion for love nor money, either.'

She had drunk most of the coffee and eaten all the biscuits Emma had and then got up to go. 'Almost forgot,' she'd said, suddenly awkward, 'me and Cook thought your ma might like a few chocs now she's better. And there's one of Cook's steak and kidney pies— just wants a warm-up—do for your dinner.'

'How lucky I am to have two such good friends,' Emma had said and meant it.

Going to the hospital on Monday, sitting quietly beside Sir Paul, she noticed him glance down at her lap where the box of chocolates sat.

'I hope that those are not for your mother?'

'Well, yes and no. Cook and Alice—from Mrs Smith-Darcy's house, you know—gave them to me to give her. I don't expect that she can have them, but she'll like to see them and she can give them to her nurses.'

He nodded. 'I examined your mother yesterday evening. I intend to have her transferred to Moreton-hampstead within the next day or so. She will remain there for two weeks at least, three if possible, so that when she returns home she will be quite fit.'

'That is good news. Thank you for arranging it,' said Emma gratefully, and wondered how she was going to visit her mother. With a car it would have been easy enough.

She would have to find out how the buses ran—probably along the highway to Exeter and then down the turn-off to Moretonhampstead halfway along it—but the buses might not connect. She had saved as much money as she could and she had her last week's wages; perhaps she could get the car from Mr Dobbs again and visit her mother once a week; it was thirty miles or so, an hour's drive…

She explained this to her mother and was relieved to see that the prospect of going to a convalescent home and starting on a normal life once more had put her in such good spirits that she made no demur when Emma suggested that she might come only once a week to see her.

'It's only for a few weeks, Emma, and I'm sure I shall have plenty to keep me occupied. I've been so well cared for here, and everyone has been so kind. Everything's all right at home? Queenie is well?'

'She's splendid and everything is fine. I'll bring you some more clothes, shall I?' She made a list and observed, 'I'll bring them tomorrow, for the professor didn't say when you were going—when there's a vacancy I expect—he just said a day or two.'

When she got up to go her mother walked part of the way with her, anxious to show how strong she had become. By the lifts they said goodbye, though, 'I'm a slow walker,' said Mrs Trent. 'It won't do to keep him waiting.'

For once, Emma was glad of Sir Paul's silence, for she had a lot to think about. They were almost at Buckfastleigh when he told her that her mother would be transferred on the day after tomorrow.

'So tomorrow will be the last day I go to the hospital?'

'Yes. Talk to Sister when you see her tomorrow; she will give you all the particulars and the phone number. Your mother will go by ambulance. The matron there is a very kind woman, there are plenty of staff and two resident doctors so your mother will be well cared for.'

'I'm sure of that. She's looking foward to going; she feels she's really getting well.'

'It has been a worrying time for you—' his voice was kind '—but I think she will make a complete recovery.'

Indoors she put the pie in the oven, fed an impatient Queenie and sat down to add up the money in her purse—enough to rent a car from Mr Dobbs on the following weekend and not much over. She ate her supper, packed a case with the clothes her mother would need and went to put the dustbin out before she went to bed.

The local paper had been pushed through the letterbox. She took it back to the kitchen and turned to the page where the few advertisements were and there, staring her in the face, was a chance of a job. It stated:

Wanted urgently—a sensible woman to help immediately for two or three weeks while present staff are ill. Someone able to cope with a small baby as well as normal household chores and able to cook.

Emma, reading it, thought that the woman wouldn't only have to be sensible, she would need to be a bundle of energy as well, but it was only for two or three weeks and it might be exactly what she was looking for. The phone number was a local one too.

Emma went to bed convinced that miracles did happen and slept soundly.

In the morning she waited with impatience until half-past eight before going round to use Mr Dobbs's phone. The voice which answered her was a woman's, shrill and agitated.

'Thank heaven—I'm at my wits' end and there's no one here. The baby's been crying all night...'

'If you would give me your address. I live in Buck-fastleigh.'

'So do I. Picket House—go past the otter sanctuary and it's at the end of the road down a turning on the left. You've got a car?'

'No, a bike. I'll come straight away, shall I?'

She listened to a jumble of incoherent thanks and, after phoning the surgery to cancel her lift with Sir Paul, hurried back to the house. Queenie, having breakfasted, was preparing to take a nap. Emma left food for her, got into her coat, tied a scarf over her head and fetched her bike. At least it wasn't raining as she pedalled briskly from one end of the little town to the other.

Picket House was a rambling old place, beautifully maintained, lying back from the lane, surrounded by a large garden. Emma skidded to the front door and halted, and before she had got off her bike it was opened.

'Come in, come in, do.' The girl wasn't much older than Emma but there the resemblance ended, for she was extremely pretty, with fair, curly hair, big blue eyes and a dainty little nose. She pulled Emma inside and then burst into tears. 'I've had a dreadful night, you have no idea. Cook's ill with flu and so is Elsie, and the nurse who's supposed to come sent a message to say that her mother's ill.'

'There's no one who could come—your mother or a sister?'

'They're in Scotland.' She dismissed them with a wave of the hand. 'And Mike, my husband, he's in America and won't be back for weeks.' She wiped her eyes and smiled a little. 'You will come and help me?'

'Yes—yes, of course. You'll want references...?'

'Yes, yes—but later will do for that. I want a bath and I've not had breakfast. To tell the truth, I'm not much of a cook.'

'The baby?' asked Emma, taking off her coat and scarf and hanging them on the elaborate hat-stand in the hall. 'A boy or a girl?'

'Oh, a boy.'

'Has he had a feed?'

'I gave him one during the night but I'm not sure if I mixed it properly; he was sick afterwards.'

'You don't feed him yourself?'

The pretty face was screwed up in horror. 'No, no, I couldn't possibly—I'm far too sensitive. Could you move in until the nurse can come?'

'I can't live here, but I'll come early in the morning and stay until the baby's last feed, if that would do?'

'I'll be alone during the night...'

'If the baby's had a good feed he should sleep for the night and I'll leave a feed ready for you to warm up.'

'Will you cook and tidy up a bit? I'm hopeless at housework.'

It seemed to Emma that now would be the time to learn about it, but she didn't say so. 'I don't know your name,' she said.

'Hervey—Doreen Hervey.'

'Emma Trent. Should we take a look at the baby before I get your breakfast?'

'Oh, yes, I suppose so. He's very small, just a month old. You're not a nurse, are you?'

'No, but I took a course in baby care and housewifery when I left school.'

They were going upstairs. 'Would you come for a hundred pounds a week?'

'Yes.' It would be two or three weeks and she could save every penny of it.

They had reached the wide landing, and from somewhere along a passage leading to the back of the house there was a small, wailing noise.

The nursery was perfection—pastel walls, a thick carpet underfoot, pretty curtains drawn back from spotless white net, the right furniture and gloriously warm. The cot was a splendid affair and Mrs Hervey went to lean over it. 'There he is,' she said unnecessarily.

He was a very small baby, with dark hair, screwed up eyes and a wide open mouth. The wails had turned to screams and he was waving miniature fists in a fury of infant rage.

'The lamb,' said Emma. 'He's wet; I'll change him. When did he have his feed? Can you remember the time?'

'I can't possibly remember; I was so tired. I suppose it was about two o'clock.'

'Is his feed in the kitchen?'

'Yes, on the table. I suppose he's hungry?'

Emma suppressed a desire to shake Mrs Hervey. 'Go and have your bath while I change him and feed him. Perhaps you could start breakfast—boil an egg and make toast?'

Mrs Hervey went thankfully away and Emma took the

sopping infant from his sopping cot. While she was at it he could be bathed; everything she could possibly need was there...

With the baby tucked under one arm, swathed in his shawl, she went downstairs presently. The tin of baby-milk was on the table in the kind of kitchen every woman dreamt of. She boiled a kettle, mixed a feed and sat down to wait while it cooled. The baby glared at her from under his shawl. Since he looked as if he would cry again at any minute she talked gently to him.

She had fed him, winded him and cuddled him close as he dropped off and there was still no sign of his mother, but presently she came, her make-up immaculate, looking quite lovely.

'Oh, good, he's gone to sleep. I'm so hungry.' She smiled widely, looking like an angel. 'I'm so glad you've come, Emma—may I call you Emma?'

'Please do,' said Emma. She had her reservations about feeling glad as she bore the baby back to his cot.

CHAPTER THREE

BY THE end of the day Emma realised that she would have her hands full for the next week or two. Mrs Hervey, no doubt a charming and good-natured woman, hadn't the least idea how to be a mother.

Over lunch she had confided to Emma that she had never had to do anything for herself—she had been pampered in succession by a devoted nanny, a doting mother and father, and then an adoring husband with money enough to keep her in the style to which she had been accustomed. 'Everyone's ill,' she had wailed. 'My old nanny ought to be here looking after me while Mike's away, but she's had to go and look after my sister's children—they've got measles. And the mother of this wretched nanny who was supposed to come. Just imagine, Emma, I came home from the nursing home and Cook and Elsie got ill the very next day!'

'You were in the nursing home for several weeks? Were you ill after the baby was born?'

'No, no. Mike arranged that so I could have plenty of time to recover before I had to plunge into normal life again.'

Emma had forborne from telling her that most women plunged back into normal life with no more help than a willing husband. She'd said cautiously, 'While I'm here I'll show you how to look after the baby and how to mix the feeds, so that when Nanny has her days off you'll know what to do.'

'Will you? How sensible you are.'

'Hasn't the baby got a name?'

'We hadn't decided on that when Mike had to go away. We called him "Baby"—I suppose he'll be Bartholemew, after Mike's father, you know. He's very rich.'

It seemed a pity, Emma had reflected, to saddle the baby with such a name for the sake of future money-bags. 'May I call him Bart?' she'd asked.

'Why not?' Mrs Hervey had cast an anxious glance at Emma. 'You're quite happy here? It's a long day...'

As indeed it was.

After the first day, ending well after nine o'clock in the evening, Emma saw that she would have to alter things a bit. A little rearranging was all that was required. Bart needed a six o'clock feed, so she agreed to make it up the evening before for his mother to warm up.

'I'll come in at eight o'clock and get your breakfast, and while you are having it I'll bath Bart and make up his feed for ten o'clock. When he's had his two o'clock feed I'll leave him with you—he'll sleep for several hours and you will be able to rest if you want to.

'I'd like to go home for an hour or two, to do the shopping and so on, but I'll be back in plenty of time to see to his evening feed and get your supper. I'll stay until nine o'clock, so that you can get ready for bed before I go, then all you need do is feed him at ten o'clock. I'll make up an extra feed in case he wakes at two o'clock.'

Mrs Hervey looked at her with her big blue eyes.

'You're an angel. Of course you must go home—and you will stay until nine o'clock?'

'Yes, of course.'

'You'll have lunch and supper with me, won't you?'

'Thank you, that would be nice. How about shopping? It wouldn't hurt Bart to be taken for an airing in his pram.'

'I'd be scared—all the traffic, and it's so far to the shops. I've always phoned for anything I want.'

'In that case, I'll take him for half an hour in the mornings when the weather's not too bad.'

'Will you? I say, I've just had such a good idea. Couldn't you take him with you in the afternoons?'

Emma had been expecting that. 'Well, no. You see, it's quite a long way and I go on my bike—I haven't anywhere to put the pram. Besides, you are his mum; he wants to be with you.'

'Oh, does he? You see, I'm not sure what to do when he cries…'

'Pick him up and see if he's wet. If he is, change him, and give him a cuddle.'

'It sounds so easy.'

'And it will be very nice if you know how to go on, so that when the nanny comes you can tell her how you want things done.'

Mrs Hervey, much struck with this idea, agreed.

It took a day or two to establish some sort of routine. Mrs Hervey was singularly helpless, not only with her son but about the running of a household; she had always had time to spend on herself and this time was now curtailed. But although she was so helpless, and not very quick to grasp anything, she had a placid nature and was very willing to learn.

The pair of them got on well and Bart, now that his

small wants were dealt with promptly, was a contented baby.

Emma phoned her mother during the week and was relieved to hear that she had settled down nicely, and when Emma explained that she had a job, just for a week or two, and might not be able to go and see her, she told her comfortably that she was quite happy and that Emma wasn't to worry.

It was on Saturday that Sir Paul Wyatt, on his way home from a conference in Bristol, decided to visit Mrs Trent. He had seen nothing of Emma in Buckfastleigh, and on the one occasion when he had given way to a wish to visit her the house had been locked up and there had been no sign of her. Staying with friends, probably, he'd decided, and didn't go again.

Mrs Trent was delighted to see him. She was making good progress and seemed happy enough. Indeed, he wondered if she might not be able to return home very shortly. Only her enthusiastic description of Emma's new job made him pause, for, if he sent her home, Emma would have to give it up, at least for a few weeks, and he suspected that the Trent household needed the money.

'Emma has a local job?' he asked kindly.

'Yes. She is able to cycle there every day. It's with a Mrs Hervey; she lives at the other end of Buckfastleigh—a very nice house, Emma says. There is a very new baby and Mrs Hervey's cook and maid are both ill and the nanny she has engaged was unable to come, so Emma's helping out until she turns up and the other two are back.'

'Mrs Hervey is a young woman, presumably?'

'Oh, yes. Her husband is away—in America I believe. Mrs Hervey seems quite lost without him.'

He agreed, that might be so.

'I'm keeping you, Professor,' she went on. 'I'm sure you want to go home to your own family. It was very kind of you to come and see me. I told Emma not to come here; from what she said I rather think that she has very little time to herself and I shall soon be home.'

'Indeed you will, Mrs Trent.'

They shook hands and she added, 'You won't be seeing her, I suppose?'

'If I do I will give her your love,' he assured her.

Fifteen minutes later he stopped the car outside his front door in the heart of Lustleigh village. The house was close to the church, and was a rambling thatched cottage, its roof at various levels, its windows small and diamond-paned. The door was arched and solid and its walls in summer and autumn were a mass of colour from the climbing plants clinging to its irregularities.

He let himself in, to be met in the narrow hall by two dogs—a Jack Russell with an impudent face and a sober golden Labrador. He bent to caress them as a door at the end of the hall was opened and his housekeeper came trotting towards him. She was short and stout with a round, pink-cheeked face, small blue eyes and a smiling mouth.

'There you are, then,' she observed, 'and high time too, if I might say so. There's as nice a dinner waiting for you as you'd find anywhere in the land.'

'Give me ten minutes, Mrs Parfitt, and I'll do it justice.'

'Had a busy day, I reckon. Time you took a bit of a holiday; though it's not my place to say so, dear knows you've earned it.' She gave an indignant snort. 'Supposed to be free of all that operating and hospital work, aren't you, for six months? And look at you, sir, working your fingers off to help out old Dr Treble, going to conferences...'

Sir Paul had taken off his coat, picked up his bag and opened a door. 'I'm rather enjoying it,' he observed mildly, and went into his study.

There was a pile of letters on his desk and the light on the answer-phone was blinking; he ignored them both and sat down at his desk and, lifting the phone's receiver, dialled a number and waited patiently for it to be answered.

Emma had soon discovered that it was impossible to get annoyed or impatient with Mrs Hervey. She had become resigned to the mess she found each morning when she arrived for work—the table in the kitchen left littered with unwashed crockery used by Mrs Hervey for the snack she fancied before she went to bed, the remnants of that snack left to solidify in the frying-pan or saucepan. But at least she had grasped the instructions for Bart's feeds, even though she made no attempt to clean anything once it had been used. She was, however, getting much better at handling her small son, and although she was prone to weep at the slightest set-back she was invariably good-natured.

Towards the end of the week Emma had suggested that it might be a good idea to take Bart to the baby clinic, or find out if there was a health visitor who would check Bart's progress.

'Absolutely not,' Mrs Hervey had said airily. 'They talked about it while I was in the nursing home but of course I said there was no need with a trained nanny already booked.'

'But the nanny isn't here,' Emma had pointed out.

'Well, you are, and she'll come soon—she said she

would.' Mrs Hervey had given her a sunny smile and begged her not to fuss but to come and inspect various baby garments which had just arrived from Harrods.

By the end of the week Emma was tired; her few hours each afternoon were just sufficient for her to look after her house, do the necessary shopping, see to Queenie and do the washing and ironing, and by the time she got home in the evening she was too tired to do more than eat a sandwich and drink a pot of tea before tumbling into bed. She was well aware that she was working for far too many hours, but she told herself it was only for a few weeks and, with the first hundred pounds swelling the woefully meagre sum in their bank account, she went doggedly on.

All the same, on Saturday evening, as nine o'clock approached, she heaved a sigh of relief. Sunday would be a day like any weekday, but perhaps by the end of another week someone—the cook or the housemaid— would be back and then her day's work would be lighter. She had been tempted once or twice to suggest that Mrs Hervey might find someone to come in each day and do some housework, but this had been dismissed with a puzzled, 'But you are managing beautifully, Emma; you're doing all the things I asked for in the advert.'

Emma had said no more—what was the use? She only hoped that Mrs Hervey would never fall on hard times; her cushioned life had hardly prepared her for that.

She was about to put on her coat when Mrs Hervey's agitated voice made her pause. She took off her coat again and went back upstairs to find her bending over Bart's cot. 'He's red in the face,' she cried. 'Look at him; he's going to have a fit, I know it!'

'He needs changing,' said Emma.

'Oh, I'm so glad you're still here.' Mrs Hervey gave her a warm smile and went to answer the phone.

She came back a few moments later. 'A visitor,' she said happily. 'He's on his way. I'll go and get the drinks ready.'

Emma, still coping with Bart's urgent needs, heard the doorbell presently, and voices. Mrs Hervey was laughing a lot; it must be someone she knew very well and was glad to see. She had, so far, refused all invitations from her friends and hadn't invited any of them to come to the house. 'I promised Mike that I'd stay quietly at home and look after Baby,' she had explained to Emma. 'As soon as Nanny is here and settled in then I shall make up for it.' Her eyes had sparkled at the thought.

Bart, now that she had made him comfortable once more, was already half-asleep; Emma was tucking him up when the door was opened and Mrs Hervey came in and, with her, Sir Paul Wyatt.

Emma's heart gave a delighted leap at the sight of him while at the same time she felt a deep annoyance; she looked a fright—even at her best she was nothing to look at, but now, at the end of the day, she wasn't worth a glance. What was he doing here anyway? She gave him a distant look and waited to see who would speak first.

It was Mrs Hervey, bubbling over with pleasure. 'Emma, this is Sir Paul Wyatt; he's a professor or something. He's Mike's oldest friend and he's come to see Bart. He didn't know that I was home—I did say that I would go to Scotland until Mike came home. Just fancy, he's turned into a GP, just for a bit while Dr Treble is away.' She turned a puzzled gaze to him. 'I thought you were a surgeon?'

'I am. This is by way of a change. Emma and I have

already met; I operated upon her mother not so long
ago.' He smiled at her across the room. 'Good evening,
Emma. You are staying here?'

'No, I'm just going home.'

'Rather late, isn't it?'

'Oh, well, that's my fault,' said Mrs Hervey cheerfully. 'Bart went all red and was roaring his head off
and Emma hadn't quite gone so she came back. I thought
he was ill.'

He lifted an enquiring eyebrow as Emma said in a no-
nonsense voice, 'He needed changing.'

He laughed. 'Oh, Doreen, when will you grow up?
The sooner Mike gets back the better!' He had gone to
lean over the cot and was looking at the sleeping infant.
'The image of his father. He looks healthy enough.' He
touched the small cheek with a gentle finger. 'Why do
you not have a nanny, and where are the servants?'

Mrs Hervey tugged at his sleeve. 'Come downstairs
and have a drink and I'll tell you.'

Emma, longing to go, saw that Bart was already
asleep.

'How do you get back?' he enquired of Emma.

'I bike—it's only a short way.' She added, in a con-
vincingly brisk tone, 'I enjoy the exercise.'

He held the door open and she followed Mrs Hervey
downstairs, got into her coat once again and heard him
telling Mrs Hervey that he could spare ten minutes and
no more. She wished them goodnight and then let herself
out of the house and pedalled furiously home.

It was already half-past nine and, although she was
hungry, she was too tired to do more than put on the
kettle for tea. She fed a disgruntled Queenie and poked
her head into the fridge and eyed its sparse contents,
trying to decide whether a boiled egg and yesterday's

loaf would be preferable to a quick bath and a cup of tea in bed.

A brisk tattoo on the door-knocker caused her to withdraw her head smartly and listen. The tattoo was repeated and she went to the door then, suddenly afraid that it was bad news of her mother. She put up the new chain and opened the door a few inches, her view quite blocked by the professor's bulk.

He said testily, 'Yes, it is I, Emma.'

'What do you want?' The door was still on the chain but she looked up into his face, half-hidden in the dark night. 'Mother?' she asked in a sudden panic.

'Your mother is well; I have seen her recently. Now, open the door, there's a good girl.'

She was too tired to argue. She opened it and he crowded into the narrow hall, his arms full.

'Fish and chips,' said Emma, suddenly famished.

'A quick and nourishing meal, but it must be eaten immediately.'

She led the way into the kitchen, took down plates from the small dresser and then paused. 'Oh, you won't want to eat fish and chips...'

'And why not? I have had no dinner this evening and I am extremely hungry.' He was portioning out the food on to the two plates while she laid the cloth and fetched knives and forks.

'I was making tea,' she told him.

'Splendid. You do not mind if I join you?'

Since he was already sitting at the table there seemed no point in objecting, and anyway, she didn't want to!

They sat opposite each other at the small table with Queenie, aroused by the delightful smell, at their feet, and for a few minutes neither of them spoke. Only when the first few mouthfuls had been eaten did Sir Paul ask, 'How long have you been with Doreen Hervey?'

Emma, gobbling chips, told him.

'And what free time do you have? It seems to me that your day is excessively long.'

'I come home each afternoon just for an hour or two...'

'To shop and wash and clean and make your bed? You are too pale, Emma; you need fresh air and a few idle hours.'

'Well, I'll get them in a week or two; the nanny said it would be only a few weeks, and Mrs Hervey told me today that the housemaid is coming back in just over a week.'

'Of course you need the money.'

He said it in such a matter-of-fact way that she said at once, 'Yes, I do, I won't be able to work for a bit when Mother comes home.' She selected a chip and bit into it. She had small very white teeth, and when she smiled and wasn't tired she looked almost pretty.

It was surprising, he reflected, what fish and chips and a pot of tea did for one. He couldn't remember when he had last had such a meal and he was glad to see that Emma's rather pale cheeks had taken on a tinge of colour.

He got up from the table, took their plates to the sink and poured the water from the kettle into the bowl.

'You can't wash up,' said Emma.

'I can and I shall. You may dry the dishes if you wish.'

'Well, really...' muttered Emma and then laughed. 'You're not a bit like a professor of surgery.'

'I am relieved to hear it. I don't spend all day and

every day bending over the operating table, you know. I have a social side to my life.'

She felt a pang of regret that she would never know what that was.

As soon as the last knife and fork had been put away he wished her a pleasant good evening and went away. She felt deflated when he had gone. 'Only because,' she explained to Queenie, for lack of any other listener, 'I don't get many people—well, many men.'

Half an hour later Sir Paul let himself into his house, to be greeted as he always was by his dogs and his housekeeper.

'Dear knows, you're a busy man, sir, but it's long past the hour any self-respecting man should be working. You'll be wanting your dinner.'

'I've dined, thank you, Mrs Parfitt. I would have phoned but there was no phone.'

'Dined? With Dr Treble?' She sniffed. 'His housekeeper is a careless one in the kitchen—I doubt you enjoyed your food.'

'Fish and chips, and I enjoyed every mouthful.'

'Not out of newspaper?' Mrs Parfitt's round face was puckered in horror.

'No, no. On a plate in the company of a young lady.'

Mrs Parfitt twinkled at him. 'Ah, I'm glad to hear it, sir. Was she pretty?'

'No.' He smiled at her. 'Don't allow your thoughts to get sentimental, Mrs Parfitt—she needed a meal.'

'Helping another of your lame dogs over the stile, were you? There's a pile of post in your study; I'll bring you a tray of coffee and some of my little biscuits.'

'Excellent. They should dispel any lingering taste of my supper.'

Mrs Parfitt was right; there were a great many letters to open and read and the answering machine to deal with. He was occupied until the early hours of the morning, when he took the dogs for a brisk walk, and saw them to their baskets and finally took himself off to bed. He hadn't thought of Emma once.

'Fancy you knowing Paul,' said Mrs Hervey, when Emma arrived in the morning. 'He's a stunner; if Mike hadn't turned up I could have fallen for him. Not that he gave me any encouragement.' She sighed. 'You see, he'll pick a suitable wife when he decides he wants one and not a minute sooner. I don't believe he's ever been in love—oh, he's dozens of girlfriends, of course, but it'll take someone special to touch his heart.'

Emma nodded. It would have to be someone like Mrs Hervey, pretty as a picture, amusing and helpless; men, Emma supposed, would like that. She thought with regret that she had never had the opportunity to be helpless. And she would never, she decided, taking a quick look in the unnecessary looking-glass in the nursery, be pretty.

That her eyes were large and thickly lashed and her hair, confined tidily in a French pleat, was long and silky, and that her mouth, though too wide, was gentle and her complexion as clear and unblemished as a baby's quite escaped her attention.

Sir Paul Wyatt, fulfilling his role of general practitioner in the middle of the following week, allowed his thoughts to dwell on just those pleasing aspects of Emma's person, only relinquishing them when the next patients came into the surgery.

Surgery finished, he went on his rounds; the inhabitants of Buckfastleigh were, on the whole, a healthy bunch and his visits were few. He drove himself home, ate his lunch, took the dogs for a walk and then got into the Rolls and drove back to Buckfastleigh again.

Emma was at home; her elderly bike was propped against the house wall and the windows were open. He knocked on the door, wondering why he had come.

She answered the door at once, an apron tied round her slender middle, her hair, loosed from its severe plait, tied back with a ribbon.

She stared up at him mutely, and he stared back with a placid face.

'Not Mother?' she said finally, and he shook his head.

'Is Mrs Hervey all right? Bart was asleep when I left.'

He nodded and she asked sharply, 'So why have you come?' She frowned. 'Do you want something?'

He smiled then. 'I am not certain about that... May I come in?'

'Sorry,' said Emma. 'Please do—I was surprised to see you...' She added unnecessarily, 'I was just doing a few chores.'

'When do you have to go back?' He was in the hall, taking up most of the space.

'Just after four o'clock to get Mrs Hervey's tea.'

He glanced at his watch. 'May we have tea here first? I'll go and get something—crumpets—while you do the dusting.'

Emma was surprised, although she agreed readily. Perhaps he had missed his lunch; perhaps surgery was earlier than usual that afternoon. She stood in the doorway and watched him drive away, and then rushed around with the duster and the carpet-sweeper before setting out the tea things. Tea would have to be in the kitchen; there was no fire laid in the sitting-room.

She fed Queenie, filled the kettle and went upstairs to do her face and pin her hair. Studying her reflection, she thought how dull she looked in her tweed skirt, blouse and—that essentially British garment—a cardigan.

She was back downstairs with minutes to spare before he returned.

It wasn't just crumpets he had brought with him—there were scones and doughnuts, a tub of butter and a pot of strawberry jam. He arranged them on a dish while she put the crumpets under the grill and boiled the kettle, all the while carrying on an undemanding conversation about nothing much so that Emma, who had felt suddenly awkward, was soothed into a pleasant feeling of ease.

They had finished the crumpets and were starting on the scones when he asked casually, 'What do you intend doing when you leave Doreen Hervey, Emma?'

'Do? Well, I'll stay at home for a bit, until Mother is quite herself again, and then I'll look for another job.'

He passed her the butter and the jam. 'You might train for something?'

'I can type and do shorthand, though I'm not very good at either, and people always need mother's helps.' She decided that it was time to change the conversation. 'I expect Mother will be on some kind of a diet?'

'Yes—small meals taken frequently, cut out vinegar and pickles and so on.' He sounded impatient. 'She will be given a leaflet when she comes home. The physicians have taken over now.' He frowned. 'Is it easy to get a job here?'

Her red herring hadn't been of much use. 'I think so. My kind of a job anyway.'

'You're wasted—bullied by selfish women and changing babies' nappies.'

'I like babies.' She added tartly, 'It's kind of you to bother, but there is no need—'

'How old are you, Emma?'

'Almost twenty-six.'

He smiled. 'Twenty-five, going on fifteen! I'm forty— do you find that old?'

'Old? Of course not. You're not yet in your prime. And you don't feel like forty, do you?'

'Upon occasion I feel ninety, but at the moment at least I feel thirty at the most!' He smiled at her and she thought what a very nice smile he had—warm and somehow reassuring. 'Have another doughnut?'

She accepted it with the forthright manner of a polite child. She was not, he reflected, in the least coy or self-conscious. He didn't search too deeply into his reasons for worrying about her future, although he admitted to the worry. It was probably because she was so willing to accept what life had to offer her.

He went presently, with a casual goodbye and no mention of seeing her again. Not that she had expected that. She cycled back to Mrs Hervey and Bart, reflecting that she was becoming quite fond of him.

It was the beginning of the third week, with another hundred pounds swelling their bank balance, when Mrs Hervey told her that the new nanny would be with them by the end of the week, and Cook and the housemaid would return in three days' time.

'And about time too,' said Mrs Hervey rather pettishly. 'I mean, three weeks just to get over flu...'

Emma held her tongue and Mrs Hervey went on, 'You'll stay until the end of the week, won't you, Emma? As soon as Cook and that girl are here I shall have a chance to go to the hairdresser. I'm desperate to get to Exeter—I need some clothes and a facial too. You'll only have Bart to look after, and Nanny comes on Friday evening. I dare say she'll want to ask your advice about Bart before you go.'

'I think,' said Emma carefully, 'that she may prefer not to do that. She's professional, you see, and I'm just a temporary help. I'm sure you will be able to tell her everything that she would want to know.'

'Will I? Write it all down for me, Emma, won't you? I never can remember Bart's feeds and what he ought to weigh.'

Certainly, once the cook and housemaid returned, life was much easier for Emma. She devoted the whole of her day to Bart, taking him for long rides in his pram, sitting with him on her lap, cuddling him and singing half-forgotten nursery rhymes while he stared up at her with his blue eyes. Cuddling was something that his mother wasn't very good at. She loved him, Emma was sure of that, but she was awkward with him. Perhaps the new nanny would be able to show Mrs Hervey how to cuddle her small son.

It was on her last day, handing over to a decidedly frosty Nanny, that she heard Sir Paul's voice in the drawing-room. She listened with half an ear to the superior young woman who was to have charge of Bart telling her of all the things she should have done, and wondered if she would see him. It seemed that she wouldn't, for presently Mrs Hervey joined them, remarking that Sir Paul had just called to see if everything was normal again.

'I asked him if he would like to see Bart but he said he hadn't the time. He was on his way to Plymouth.' She turned to the nanny. 'You've had a talk with Emma? Wasn't it fortunate that she was able to come and help

me?' She made a comic little face. 'I'm not much good
with babies.'

'I'm accustomed to take sole charge, Mrs Hervey; you
need have no further worries about Bart. Tomorrow, perhaps, we might have a little talk and I will explain my
duties to you.'

It should surely be the other way round, thought
Emma. But Mrs Hervey didn't seem to mind.

'Oh, of course. I'm happy to leave everything to you.
You're ready to go, Emma? Say goodbye to Bart; he's
got very fond of you...'

A remark which annoyed Nanny, for she said quite
sharply that the baby was sleeping and shouldn't be disturbed. So Emma had to content herself with looking at
him lying in his cot, profoundly asleep, looking like a
very small cherub.

She would miss him.

She bade Nanny a quiet goodbye and went downstairs
with Mrs Hervey and got on her bike, warmed by that
lady's thanks and the cheque in her pocket. Three hundred pounds would keep them going for quite some time,
used sparingly with her mother's pension.

When she got home, she took her bike round to the
shed, went indoors and made some supper for Queenie,
and boiled an egg for herself. She felt sad that the job
was finished, but a good deal of the sadness was because
she hadn't seen the professor again.

There was a letter from her mother in the morning, telling her that she would be brought home by ambulance
in two days' time. How nice, she wrote, that Emma's
job was finished just in time for her return. Emma wondered how she had known that, and then forgot about it
as she made plans for the next two days.

It was pleasant to get up the next morning and know that she had the day to herself. It was Sunday, of course, so she wouldn't be able to do any shopping, but there was plenty to do in the house—the bed to make up, wood and coal to be brought in, the whole place to be dusted and aired. And, when that was done, she sat down and made a shopping list.

Bearing in mind what Sir Paul had said about diet, she wrote down what she hoped would be suitable and added flowers and one or two magazines, Earl Grey tea instead of the economical brand they usually drank, extra milk and eggs—the list went on and on, but for once she didn't care. Her mother was coming home and that was a cause for extravagance.

She had the whole of Monday morning in which to shop, and with money in her purse she enjoyed herself, refusing to think about the future, reminding herself that it would soon be the tourist season again and there were always jobs to be found. It didn't matter what she did so long as she could be at home.

Her mother arrived during the afternoon, delighted to be at home again, protesting that she felt marvellous, admiring the flowers and the tea-tray on a small table by the lighted fire in the sitting-room. Emma gave the ambulance driver tea and biscuits, received an envelope with instructions as to her mother's diet and went back to her mother.

Mrs Trent certainly looked well; she drank her weak tea and ate the madeira cake Emma had baked and settled back in her chair. 'Now, tell me all the news, Emma. What was this job like? Were you happy? A nice change looking after a baby?'

Emma recounted her days, making light of the long hours. 'It was a very nice job,' she declared, 'and I earned three hundred pounds, so I can stay at home for as long as you want me to.'

They talked for the rest of that afternoon and evening, with Queenie sitting on Mrs Trent's lap and finally trailing upstairs with her to curl up on her bed.

Emma, taking her some warm milk and making sure that she was comfortable before she went to bed herself, felt a surge of relief at the sight of her mother once more in her own bed. The future was going to be fine, she told herself as she kissed her mother goodnight.

CHAPTER FOUR

EMMA and her mother settled down into a quiet routine: gentle pottering around the house, short walks in the afternoon, pleasant evenings round the fire at the end of the day. For economy's sake, Emma shared her mother's small, bland meals, and found herself thinking longingly of the fish and chips Sir Paul had brought to the house.

There was no sign of him, of course, and it wasn't likely that she would see him again; the new doctor had come to take over from Dr Treble and the professor had doubtless taken up his normal life again. She speculated a bit about that, imagining him stalking the wards with a bunch of underlings who hung on to any words of wisdom he might choose to utter and watched with awe while he performed some complicated operation. And his private life? Her imagination ran riot over that—married to some beautiful young woman—she would have to be beautiful, he wouldn't look at anyone less—perhaps with children—handsome little boys and pretty little girls. If he wasn't married he would certainly have any number of women-friends and get asked out a great deal—dinner parties and banquets and evenings at the theatre and visits to London.

A waste of time, she told herself time and again—she would forget all about him. But that wasn't easy, because her mother talked about him a great deal although, when pumped by Emma, she was unable to tell her anything about his private life.

Mrs Trent had been home for a week when he came to see her. Emma had seen the Rolls draw up from her mother's bedroom window and had hurried down to open the door, forgetting her unmade-up face and her hair bunched up anyhow on top of her head. It was only as she opened the door that she remembered her appearance, so that she met his faintly amused look with a frown and her feelings so plain on her face that he said to her at once, 'I do apologise for coming unexpectly, but I had half an hour to spare and I wanted to see how your mother was getting on.'

'Hello,' said Emma gruffly, finding her voice and her manners. 'Please come in; she will be glad to see you.'

She led the way into the little sitting-room. 'I was going to make Mother's morning drink and have some coffee. Would you like a cup?' She gave him a brief glance. 'Shall I take your coat?'

'Coffee would be delightful.' He took off his overcoat and flung it over a chair and went to take Mrs Trent's hand, which gave Emma the chance to escape. She galloped up to her room, powdered her nose, pinned up her hair and tore downstairs again to make the coffee and carry it in presently, looking her usual neat self.

Sir Paul, chatting with her mother, looked at her from under his lids and hid a smile, steering the conversation with effortless ease towards trivial matters. It was only when they had finished their coffee that he asked Mrs Trent a few casual questions. He seemed satisfied with her answers and presently took his leave.

As he shook hands with the older woman she asked, 'Are you still working here as a GP? Has the new doctor arrived?'

'Several days ago; he will be calling on you very shortly, I have no doubt.'

'So we shan't see you again? I owe you so much, Sir Paul.'

'It is a great satisfaction to me to see you on your feet again, Mrs Trent. Don't rush things, will you? You're in very capable hands.' He glanced at Emma, who had her gaze fixed on his waistcoat and didn't meet his eye.

When he had driven away Mrs Trent said, 'I'm sorry we shan't see him again. I felt quite safe with him…'

'I expect the new doctor is just as kind as Dr Treble. I'm sure he'll come and see you in a day or two, Mother.'

Which he did—a pleasant, youngish man who asked the same questions that Sir Paul had asked, assured Emma that her mother was making excellent progress and suggested that she might go to the surgery in a month's time for a check-up.

'No need really,' he said cheerfully. 'But I should like to keep an eye on you for a little while.' As Emma saw him to the door he observed, 'I'm sure you're looking after your mother very well; it's fortunate that you are living here with her.' It was a remark which stopped her just in time from asking him when he thought it would be suitable for her to look for a job again.

The days slid past, each one like the previous; Mrs Trent was content to knit and read and go for short walks, and Emma felt a faint prick of unease. Surely by now her mother should be feeling more energetic? She was youngish still—nowadays most people in their fifties were barely middle-aged and still active—but her mother seemed listless, and disinclined to exert herself.

The days lengthened and winter began to give way

reluctantly to spring, but Mrs Trent had no inclination to go out and about. Emma got Mr Dobbs to drive them to the surgery, when a month was up, after reminding her mother that it was time she saw the doctor again.

She had already spoken to him on Mr Dobbs's phone, voicing her vague worries and feeling rather silly since there was nothing definite to tell him, but he was kindness itself as he examined Mrs Trent.

He said finally, 'You're doing very well, Mrs Trent—well enough to resume normal life once more. I'll see about some surgical stockings for you—you do have a couple of varicose veins. Recent, are they?'

'Oh, yes, but they don't bother me really. I'm not on my feet all that much.' Mrs Trent laughed. 'I'm getting rather lazy...'

'Well, don't get too lazy; a little more exercise will do you good, I think. The operation was entirely successful and there is no reason why you shouldn't resume your normal way of life.' He gave her an encouraging smile. 'Come and see me in a month's time and do wear those stockings—I'll see you get them.'

'A nice young man,' declared Mrs Trent as they were driven home by Mr Dobbs and Emma agreed, although she had the feeling that he had thought her over-fussy about her mother. Still, he had said that her mother was quite well again, excepting for those veins...

It was several days later, as she was getting their tea, that she heard her mother call out and then the sound of her falling. She flew to the sitting-room and found her mother lying on the floor, and she knew before she picked up her hand that there would be no pulse.

'Mother,' said Emma, and even though it was useless she put a cushion under her head before she tore out of the house to Mr Dobbs and the phone.

An embolism, the doctor said, a pulmonary embolism, sudden and fatal. Emma said, in a voice which didn't sound like hers, 'Varicose veins—it was a blood clot.' She saw his surprised look. 'I've done my First Aid.' She raised anguished eyes to his. 'Couldn't you have known?'

He shook his head. 'No, there were no symptoms and varicose veins are commonplace; one always bears in mind that a clot might get dislodged, but there is usually some warning.'

'She wouldn't have known?'

'No, I'm certain of that.'

There was no one to turn to, no family or very close friends, although the neighbours were kind—cooking her meals she couldn't eat, offering to help. They had liked her mother and they liked her and she was grateful, thanking them in a quiet voice without expression, grief a stone in her chest.

They came to the funeral too, those same neighbors, and the doctor, Cook and Alice from Mrs Smith-Darcy's house, taking no notice of that lady's orders to remain away. Mrs Hervey was there too, and kind Mr Dobbs. The only person Emma wanted to see was absent—Sir Paul Wyatt wasn't there, and she supposed that he had no reason to be there anyway. That he must know she was certain, for the doctor had told her that he had written to him...

There was no money, of course, and no will. She remembered her mother telling her laughingly that when she was sixty she would make one, but in any case there was almost nothing to leave—the house and the furniture and a few trinkets.

Emma, during the next few empty days, pondered her future. She would sell the house if she could find a small

flat in Plymouth, and train properly as a shorthand typist
and then find a permanent job. She had no real wish to
go to Plymouth but if she went to Exeter, a city she
knew and loved, she might meet Sir Paul—something,
she told herself, she didn't wish to do. Indeed, she didn't
want to see him again.

A new life, she decided, and the sooner the better.
Thirty wasn't all that far off, and by then she was de-
termined to have built herself a secure future. 'At least
I've got Queenie,' she observed to the empty sitting-
room as she polished and dusted, quite unnecessarily because the house was clean, but it filled the days. She
longed to pack her things and settle her future at once,
but there were all the problems of unexpected death to
unravel first, so she crammed her days with hard work
and cried herself to sleep each night, hugging Queenie
for comfort, keeping her sorrow to herself.

People were very kind—calling to see how she was,
offering companionship, suggesting small outings—and
to all of them she showed a cheerful face and gave the
assurance that she was getting along splendidly and
making plans for the future, and they went away, relieved that she was coping so well.

'Of course, Emma has always been such a sensible
girl,' they told each other, deceived by her calm manner.

Ten days after the funeral, her small affairs not yet settled, she was in the kitchen, making herself an early
morning cup of tea and wondering how much longer she
would have to wait before she could put the house up
for sale. She would keep most of the furniture, she
mused, sitting down at the kitchen table, only to be interrupted by a bang on the door-knocker. It must be the
postman, earlier than usual, but perhaps there would be

something interesting in the post. The unbidden thought that there might be a letter from Sir Paul passed through her mind as she opened the door.

It wasn't a letter from him but he himself in person, looming in the doorway and, before she could speak, inside the house, squashed up against her in the narrow little hall.

At the sight of him she burst into tears, burying her face in the tweed of his jacket without stopping to think what she was doing, only aware of the comfort of his arms around her.

He said gently, 'My poor girl. I didn't know—I've been in America and only got back yesterday evening. I was told what had happened by your doctor. He wrote— but by the time I had read his letter it was too late to come to you. I am so very sorry.'

'There wasn't anyone,' said Emma, between great heaving sobs. 'Everyone was so kind...' It was a muddled remark, which he rightly guessed referred to his absence. He let her cry her fill and presently, when the sobs became snivels, he offered a large white linen handkerchief.

'I'm here now,' he said cheerfully, 'and we'll have breakfast while you tell me what happened.' He gave her an avuncular pat on the back and she drew away from him, feeling ashamed of her outburst but at the same time aware that the hard stone of her grief had softened to a gentle sorrow.

'I'm famished,' said Sir Paul in a matter-of-fact voice which made the day normal again. 'I'll lay the table while you cook.'

'I must look a fright. I'll go and do something to my face...'

He studied her with an impersonal look which she

found reassuring. Not a fright, he reflected, but the face far too pale, the lovely eyes with shadows beneath them and the clear skin blotched and pinkened with her tears. 'It looks all right to me,' he told her and knew that, despite the tearstains, she was feeling better.

'As long as you don't mind,' she said rather shyly, and got out the frying-pan. 'Will fried eggs and fried bread do?' she asked. 'I'm afraid there isn't any bacon...'

'Splendidly. Where do you keep the marmalade?'

They sat down eventually, facing each other across the kitchen table and Emma, who had had no appetite for days, discovered that she was hungry. It wasn't until they had topped off the eggs with toast and marmalade that Sir Paul allowed the conversation to become serious.

'What are your plans?' he wanted to know, when he had listened without interruption to her account of her mother's death.

'I'll have to sell this house. I thought I'd find a small flat in Plymouth and take a course in office management and then get a proper job. I've enough furniture and I'll have Queenie.'

'Is there no money other than the proceeds from the house?'

'Well, no, there isn't. Mother's pension won't be paid any more of course.' She added hastily, anxious to let him see that she was able to manage very well, 'I can put the house up for sale just as soon as I'm allowed to. There are still some papers and things. They said they'd let me know.'

'And is that what you would like to do, Emma?'

'Yes, of course.' She caught his eye and added honestly, 'I don't know what else to do.'

He smiled at her across the table. 'Will you marry me, Emma?'

Her mouth dropped open. 'Marry you? You're joking!'

'Er—no, I have never considered marriage a joke.'

'Why do you want to marry me? You don't know anything about me—and I'm plain and not a bit interesting. Besides, you don't—don't love me.'

'I know enough about you to believe that you would make me an admirable wife and, to be truthful, I have never considered you plain. As for loving you, I am perhaps old-fashioned enough to consider that mutual liking and compatibility and the willingness to make a good marriage are excellent foundations for happiness. Since the circumstances are unusual we will marry as soon as possible and get to know each other at our leisure.'

'But your family and your friends...?' She saw his lifted eyebrows and went on awkwardly, 'What I mean is, I don't think I'm used to your kind of life.' She waved a hand round the little kitchen. 'I don't expect it's like this.'

He said evenly, 'I live in a thatched cottage at Lustleigh and I have an elderly housekeeper and two dogs. My mother and father live in the Cotswolds and I have two sisters, both married. I'm a consultant at the Exeter hospitals and I frequently go to London, where I am a consultant at various hospitals. I go abroad fairly frequently, to lecture and operate, but at present I have taken a sabbatical, although I still fulfil one or two appointments.'

'Aren't you too busy to have a wife? I mean—' she frowned, trying to find the right words '—you lead such a busy life.'

'When I come home in the evenings it will be pleasant to find you there, waiting to listen to my grumbles if things haven't gone right with my day, and at the weekends I will have a companion.'

'You don't—that is, you won't mind me not loving you?'

'I think,' he said gently, 'that we might leave love out of it, don't you?' He smiled a tender smile, which warmed her down to the soles of her feet. 'We like each other, don't we? And that's important.'

'You might fall in love with someone...'

She wasn't looking at him, otherwise she would have seen his slow smile.

'So might you—a calculated risk which we must both take.' He smiled again, completely at ease. 'I'll wash up and tidy things away while you go and pack a bag.'

'A bag? What for?'

'You're coming back with me. And while Mrs Parfitt fattens you up and the moor's fresh air brings colour into your cheeks you can decide what you want to do.' When she opened her mouth to speak he raised a hand. 'No, don't argue, Emma. I've no intention of leaving you alone here. Later you can tell me what still has to be settled about the house and furniture and I'll deal with the solicitor. Are the bills paid?'

He was quite matter-of-fact about it and she found herself telling him that there were still a few outstanding. 'But everyone said they'd wait until the house was sold.'

He nodded. 'Leave it to me, if you will. Now, run along and get some things packed. Has Queenie got a basket?'

'Yes, it's beside the dresser.'

She went meekly upstairs, and only as she was packing did she reflect that he was behaving in a high-handed fashion, getting his own way without any effort. That, she reminded herself, was because she was too tired and unhappy to resist him. She was thankful to leave everything to him, but once she had pulled herself together she would convince him that marrying him was quite out of the question.

And, since he didn't say another word about it as he drove back to Lustleigh, she told herself that he might have made the suggestion on the spur of the moment and was even now regretting it.

It was a bright morning and cold, but spring was definitely upon them. Lustleigh was a pretty village and a pale sun shone on its cottages. It shone on Sir Paul's home too and Emma, getting out of the car, fell in love with the house at first glance.

'Oh, how delightful. It's all nooks and crannies, isn't it?'

He had a hand under her elbow, urging her to the door. 'It has been in the family for a long time, and each generation has added a room or a chimney-pot or another window just as the fancy took it.' He opened the door and Mrs Parfitt came bustling down the curving staircase at the back of the hall.

'God bless my soul, so you're back, sir.'

She cast him a reproachful look and he said quickly, 'I got back late last night and went straight to the hospital and, since it was already after midnight and I wanted to go to Buckfastleigh as early as possible, I didn't come home. They put me up there.' He still had his hand on Emma's arm. 'Mrs Parfitt, I've brought a guest who will stay with us for a little while. Miss Trent's mother died recently and she needs a break. Emma, this is my housekeeper, Mrs Parfitt.'

Emma shook hands, conscious of sharp, elderly eyes looking her over.

'I hope I won't give you too much extra work...'

Mrs Parfitt had approved of what she saw. All in good time, she promised herself, she would discover the whys and wherefores. 'A pleasure to have someone in the house, miss, for Sir Paul is mostly away from home or shut in that study of his—he might just as well be in the middle of the Sahara for all I see of him!'

She chuckled cosily. 'I'll bring coffee into the sitting-room, shall I, sir? And get a room ready for Miss Trent?'

Sir Paul took Emma's coat and opened a door, urging her ahead of him. The room was long and low, with small windows overlooking the narrow street and glass doors opening on to the garden at the far end. He went past her to open them and let in the dogs, who danced around, delighted to see him.

'Come and meet Kate and Willy,' he invited, and Emma crossed the room and offered a balled fist.

'Won't they mind Queenie?' she wanted to know.

'Not in the least, and Mrs Parfitt will be delighted; her cat died some time ago and she is always talking of getting a kitten—Queenie is much more suitable. I'll get her, and they can get used to each other while we have our coffee.'

While he was gone she looked around the room. Its walls were irregular and there were small windows on each side of the inglenook, and a set of heavy oak beams supporting the ceiling. The walls were white but there was no lack of colour in the room—the fine old carpet almost covered the wood floor, its russets and faded blues toning with the velvet curtains. There were book-shelves crammed with books, several easy-chairs, and a vast sofa drawn up to the fire and charming pie-crust tables holding reading lamps—a delightful lived-in room.

She pictured it in mid-winter, when the wind whistled from the moor and snow fell; with the curtains drawn and a fire roaring up the chimney one would feel safe and secure and content. For the first time since her mother's death she felt a small spark of happiness.

Sir Paul, coming in with Queenie under his arm, disturbed her thoughts and saw them reflected in her face. He said casually, 'You like this room? Let us see if Queenie approves of it… No, don't worry about the dogs—they'll not touch her.'

Mrs Parfitt came in to bring the coffee then, and they sat drinking it, watching the dogs, obedient to their master, sitting comfortably while Queenie edged round them and finally, to Emma's surprise, sat down and washed herself.

'The garden is walled—she won't be able to get out; she'll be quite at home in a few days. I've taken your bag upstairs; I expect you would like to unpack before lunch. This afternoon we'll walk round the village so that you can find your way about. I'll take the dogs for a run and see you at lunch.'

Emma, soothed by the room and content to have someone to tell her how to order her day, nodded. It was like being in a dream after the loneliness of the last week or two. It wouldn't last, of course, for she had no intention of marrying Sir Paul. But for the moment she was happy to go on dreaming.

She was led away presently, up the charming little staircase and on to a landing with passages leading from it in all directions.

'A bit of a jumble,' said Mrs Parfitt cheerfully, 'but you'll soon find your way around. I've put you in a nice quiet room overlooking the garden. Down this passage and up these two steps. The door's a bit narrow...'

Which it was—solid oak like the rest of the doors in the cottage and opening into a room with a large circle of windows taking up all of one wall. There was a balcony beyond them with a wrought-iron balustrade and a sloping roof. 'For your little cat,' explained Mrs Parfitt. 'I dare say you like to have her with you at night? I always had my Jenkin—such a comfort he was!'

'How thoughtful of you, Mrs Parfitt. I hope you'll like Queenie; she's really very good.'

'Bless you, miss, I like any cat.' She trotted over to another door by the bed. 'The bathroom's here and mind the step down, and if there's anything you need you just say so. You'll want to hang up your things now. Lunch is at one o'clock, but come downstairs when you're ready and sit by the fire.'

When she had gone Emma looked around her; the room had uneven walls so that the bay window took up the longest of them. There was a small fireplace in the centre of one short wall and the bedhead was against the wall facing the window. That was irregular too, and the fourth wall had a deep-set alcove into which the dressing-table fitted. She ran a finger along its surface, delighting in the golden brown of the wood.

It was a cosy room, despite the awkwardness of its shape, and delightfully furnished in muted pinks and blues. She unpacked her things and laid them away in the tallboy, and hung her dress in the cupboard concealed in one of the walls. She had brought very little with her—her sensible skirt and blouses, her cardigan and this one dress. She tidied away her undies, hung up her dressing-gown and sat down before the dressing-table.

Her reflection wasn't reassuring and that was partly her fault, for she hadn't bothered much with her appearance during the two weeks since her mother had died—something she would have to remedy. She did her face and brushed her hair and pinned it into its neat French pleat and went downstairs, peering along the various passages as she went.

It was indeed a delightful house, and although Sir Paul had called it a cottage it was a good deal larger than that. There was no sign of him when she reached the hall but Mrs Parfitt popped her head round a door.

'He won't be long, miss. Come into the kitchen if you've a mind. Your little cat's here, as good as gold, sitting in the warm. Taken to us like a duck to water, she has.'

Indeed, Queenie looked as though she had lived there all her life, stretched out before the Aga.

'You don't mind her being here? In your kitchen?'

'Bless you, miss, whatever harm could she do? Just wait while I give the soup a stir and I'll show you the rest of it...'

She opened a door and led the way down a short passage. 'This bit of the house Sir Paul's grandfather added; you can't see it from the lane. There's a pantry—' she opened another door '—and a wash-house opposite and all mod cons—Sir Paul saw to that. And over here there's what was the stillroom; I use it for bottled fruit and jam and pickles. I make those myself. Then there's this cubby-hole where the shoes are cleaned and the dogs' leads and such like are kept. If ever you should want a good thick coat there's plenty hanging there—boots too.'

She opened the door at the end of the passage. 'The back garden, miss; leastways, the side of it with a gate into the path which leads back to the lane.' She gave a chuckle. 'Higgledy-piggledy, as you might say, but you'll soon find your way around.'

As she spoke the gate opened and Sir Paul and the dogs came through.

'Ready for lunch?' he wanted to know, and swept Emma back with him to the sitting-room. 'A glass of sherry? It will give you an appetite.'

It loosened her tongue too, so that over Mrs Parfitt's delicious lunch she found herself answering his carefully casual questions and even, from time to time, letting slip some of her doubts and fears about the future, until she remembered with a shock that he had offered her a future and here she was talking as though he had said nothing.

He made no comment, but began to talk about the village and the people living in it. It was obvious to her that he was attached to his home, although according to Mrs Parfitt he was away a good deal.

He took her round the house after lunch. There was a small sitting-room at the front of the cottage, with his study behind it. A dining-room was reached through a short passage and, up several steps to one side of the hall, there was a dear little room most comfortably furnished and with rows of bookshelves, filled to overflowing. Emma could imagine sitting there by the fire, reading her fill.

There was a writing-desk under the small window, with blotter, writing-paper and envelopes neatly arranged upon it, and the telephone to one side. One could sit there and write letters in comfort and peace, she thought. Only there was no one for her to write to. Well, there was Mr Dobbs, although he was always so busy he probably wouldn't have time to read a letter, and she hardly thought that Mrs Hervey would be inter-

ested. Cook and Alice, of course, but they would prefer
postcards...

Sir Paul had been watching her. 'You like this room?'

She nodded. 'I like the whole cottage; it's like home.'

'It is home, Emma.'

She had no answer to that.

She was given no time to brood. During the next few
days he walked her over the moor, taking the dogs, bun-
dling her into one of the elderly coats by the back door,
marching her along, mile after mile, not talking much,
and when they got home Mrs Parfitt had delicious meals
waiting for them, so that between the good food and
hours in the open air she was blissfully tired at the end
of each day, only too willing to accept Sir Paul's suggestion that she should go early to bed—to fall asleep
the moment her head touched the pillow.

On Sunday he took her to church. St John's dated
from the thirteenth century, old and beautiful, and a mere
stone's throw from the cottage. Wearing the dress under
her winter coat, and her only hat—a plain felt which did
nothing for her—Emma sat beside him in a pew in the
front of the church, and watched him read the lesson,
surprised that he put on a pair of glasses to do so, but
enthralled by his deep, unhurried voice. Afterwards she
stood in the church porch while he introduced her to the
rector and his wife, and several people who stopped to
speak to him.

They were friendly, and if they were curious they
were far too well-mannered to show it. They all gave
them invitations to come for a drink or to dine, prom-
ising to phone and arrange dates, chorusing that they
must get to know Emma while she was in Lustleigh.

'We are always glad to see a new face,' declared a

talkative middle-aged woman. 'And as for you, Paul, we see you so seldom that you simply must come.'

He replied suitably but, Emma noted, made no promises. That made sense too; their curiosity would be even greater if she were to return home and never be seen again there. Sir Paul would deal with that without fuss, just as he did everything else. She remained quiet, smiling a little and making vague remarks when she had to.

After Sunday lunch, sitting by the fire, the Sunday papers strewn around, the dogs at Sir Paul's feet and Queenie on her lap, Emma said suddenly, 'You have a great many friends...'

He looked at her over his glasses and then took them off. 'Well, I have lived here for a number of years, and my parents before me, and their parents before them. We aren't exactly cut off from the world but we are a close-knit community.' He added casually, 'I believe you will fit in and settle down very well here.'

His gaze was steady and thoughtful, and after a moment she said, 'I don't understand why you want me to marry you.'

'I have given you my reasons. They are sound and sensible. I am not a young man, to make decisions lightly, Emma.'

'No, I'm sure of that. But it isn't just because you're sorry for me?'

'No, certainly not. That would hardly be a good foundation for a happy marriage.'

He smiled at her and she found herself smiling too. 'We might quarrel...'

'I should be very surprised if we didn't from time to time—which wouldn't matter in the least since we are both sensible enough to make it up afterwards. We are bound to agree to differ about a number of things—life would be dull if we didn't.'

Early the following week he drove her to Buck-fastleigh. 'You're having coffee with Doreen Hervey,' he told her. 'Unless you want to come with me to the solicitor and house agent. Will you stay with her until I fetch you?'

'Should I go with you?'

'Not unless you wish to. From what you have told me, everything is settled and you can sell your house. The solicitor has already been in contact with the house agent, hasn't he? It's just a question of tying up the ends. Would you like to go there and see if there's anything you want to keep? There's plenty of room at the cottage.'

'You're talking as though we are going to be married.'

For a moment he covered her clasped hands with one of his. He said quietly, 'Say yes, Emma, and trust me.'

She turned her head to gaze at his calm face. He was not looking at her, but watching the road ahead. Of course she trusted him; he was the nicest person she had ever met, and the kindest.

'I do trust you,' she told him earnestly, 'and I'll marry you and be a good wife.'

He gave her a quick glance—so quick that she hadn't time to puzzle over the look on his face. She dismissed it, suddenly filled quite joyously with quiet content.

CHAPTER FIVE

EMMA and Paul had a lot to talk about as he drove back later that day. Everything, he assured her, was arranged; it was now only a question of selling the house.

He had settled the few debts, paid the outstanding bills and returned to Doreen Hervey's house, where he found Emma in the nursery, hanging over Bart's cot, heedless of Nanny's disapproval.

Mrs Hervey, sitting meekly in the chair Nanny had offered, had been amused. 'Wait till you've got one of your own,' she had said.

Emma had turned her face away, her cheeks warm, and listened thankfully to his easy, 'One would imagine that you were worn to a thread looking after Bart, Doreen. When will Mike be home?'

He had taken her to her house then, and helped her decide which small keepsakes she wished to have—a few pieces of silver, some precious china, her mother's little Victorian work table, her father's silver tankard, photos in old silver frames.

Standing in the small sitting-room, she had asked diffidently, 'Would you mind if Mr Dobbs and Cook and Alice came and chose something? They were very kind to me and to Mother…'

'Of course. We'll take the car and fetch them now.'

'Mrs Smith-Darcy will never let them come.'

'Leave it to me. You stay here and collect the things you want while I bring them here.'

She didn't know what he had said but they were all there within twenty minutes, and she had left them to choose what they wanted.

'If I could have some of Mrs Trent's clothes?' Alice had whispered. Alice was the eldest of numerous children, whose wages went straight into the family purse. She had gone away delighted, with Cook clutching several pictures she had fancied. As for Mr Dobbs, he had had an eye on the clock in the kitchen for a long time, he had told her.

Sir Paul had taken them all back and mentioned casually on his return that he had arranged to send everything but the furniture to a charity shop. Emma had been dreading packing up her mother's clothes and the contents of the linen cupboard. She had thanked him with gratitude.

He had popped her back into the car then, taken her to Buckland in the Moor and given her lunch at the country hotel there. She had been conscious that her first sharp grief had given way to a gentle sorrow and she had been able to laugh and talk and feel again. She had tried to thank him then. 'I told you that I would never be able to repay you for all you did for Mother, and now I'm doubly in your debt.'

He had smiled his kind smile. 'Shall we cry quits? After all, I'm getting a wife, am I not? And I fancy the debt should be mine.'

That evening, as they sat round the fire, with the dogs and Queenie sprawling at their feet, he suggested that they might go to Exeter on the following day. 'You have plenty of money now,' he reminded her, and when she told him that she had only a few pounds he said, 'You forget your house. Supposing I settle any bills for the present and you pay me when it is sold?'

'I already owe you money for the solicitor and all these debts...'

'You can easily repay those also, but all in good time. I'm sure that the house will sell well enough.'

'Thank you so much, then; I do need some clothes.'

'I have yet to meet a woman who didn't. At the same time we might decide on a date for our wedding. There is no point in waiting, is there? Will you think about it and let me know what you would like to do?'

When she didn't reply he went on quietly, 'Supposing we go along and see the vicar? He can read the banns; that will give you three weeks to decide on a date. It will also give you a breathing-space to think things over.'

'You mean if I should want to back out?'

'Precisely.' He was smiling at her.

'I'll not do that,' said Emma.

She was uncertain what to buy and sat up in bed that night making a list. Good clothes, of course, suitable for the wife of a consultant surgeon and at the same time wearable each day in the country. 'Tweeds,' she wrote. 'Suit and a top-coat'—even though spring was well settled in it could be cold on the moor.

One or two pretty dresses, she thought, and undies, shoes—and perhaps she could find a hat which actually did something for her. She would need boots and slippers—and should she look for something to wear in the evenings? Did those people she'd met at the church give parties or rather grand dinners?

She asked Paul at breakfast. He was a great help.

'The dinner parties are usually formal—black tie and so on, short frocks for the ladies. I suppose because we tend to make our own amusements, celebrating birthdays and so on. But more often, as far as I remember, the ladies wear pretty dresses. You'll need a warm wrap of some kind, though, for the evening. It'll stay chilly here for some time yet.' He looked across at her list. 'Don't forget a warm dressing-gown and slippers.'

'I need rather a lot…'

'You have plenty of money coming to you.'

'How much should I spend?'

He named a sum which left her open-mouthed. 'But that's hundreds and hundreds!'

Poker-faced, he observed that good clothes lasted a long time and were more economical in the long run.

'You really don't mind lending me the money?'

'No. I'll come with you and write the cheques. If you outrun the constable, I'll warn you.'

Thus reassured, Emma plunged into her day's shopping. She would have gone to one of the department stores but Paul took her instead to several small, elegant and very expensive boutiques. Even with a pause for coffee, by lunchtime she had acquired a tweed suit, a cashmere top-coat—its price still made her feel a little faint—more skirts, blouses and sweaters, a windproof jacket to go with them, and two fine wool dresses.

When she would have chosen shades which she considered long-wearing he had suggested something more colourful—plaids, a dress in garnet-red, another in turquoise and various shades of blue, silk blouses in old rose, blue and green, and a dress for the dinner parties— a tawny crêpe, deceptively simple.

He took her to lunch then. Watching her crossing through her list, he observed, 'A good waterproof, don't

you think? Then I'll collect the parcels and go to the car
and leave you to buy the rest. Will an hour be enough?'

'Yes, oh, yes.' She paused, wondering how she should
tell him that she had barely enough money to buy stockings, let alone undies and a dressing-gown.

'You'll need some money.' He was casual about it,
handing her a roll of notes. 'If it isn't enough we can
come again tomorrow.'

They bought the raincoat, and a hat to go with it,
before he left her at a department store. 'Don't worry
about the time; I'll wait,' he told her, and waited until
she was inside.

Before she bought anything she would have to count
the notes he had given her. There was no one else in the
Ladies, and she took the roll out of her handbag. The
total shocked her—she could have lived on it for
months. At the same time it presented the opportunity
for her to spend lavishly.

Which she did. Might as well be hung for a sheep as
for a lamb, she reflected, choosing silk and lace undies,
a quilted dressing-gown, and matching up stockings with
shoes and the soft leather boots she had bought. Even
so, there was still money in her purse. Laden with her
purchases, she left the shop and found Paul waiting for
her.

He took her packages from her. 'Everything you need
for the time being?' he asked.

'For years,' she corrected him. 'I've had a lovely day,
Paul; you have no idea. There's a lot of money left
over...'

'Keep it. I'm sure you'll need it.' He glanced side-
ways at her. 'Before we marry,' he added.

It was at breakfast the next morning that he told her that
he would be away for a few days. 'I have an appointment

in Edinburgh which I must keep,' he told her. 'If you want to go to Exeter for more shopping ask Truscott at the garage to drive you there and bring you back here. I'll have a word with him before I go.'

'Thank you.' She was very conscious of disappointment but all she said was, 'May I take the dogs out?'

'Of course. I usually walk them to Lustleigh Cleave in the early morning. If it's clear weather you'll enjoy a good walk on the moor.'

'I can christen the new tweeds,' said Emma soberly. He wouldn't be there to see them; she had been looking forward to astonishing him with the difference in her appearance when she was well-dressed. That would have to wait now. 'You're leaving today?'

'In an hour or so. Mrs Parfitt will look after you, Emma, but feel free to do whatever you like; this house will be your home as well as mine.'

He had gone by mid-morning, and when she had had coffee with Mrs Parfitt she went to her room with Queenie and tried on her new clothes.

They certainly made a difference; their colours changed her ordinary features to near prettiness and their cut showed off her neat figure. It was a pity that Paul wasn't there to see the chrysalis changing into a butterfly. She had to make do with Queenie.

She had to admit that by teatime, even though she had filled the rest of the day by taking the dogs for a long walk, she was missing him, which was, of course, exactly what he had intended.

Mrs Parfitt, when Emma asked her the next day, had no idea when he would be back. 'Sir Paul goes off for days at a time,' she explained to Emma. 'He goes to other hospitals, and abroad too. Does a lot of work in

London, so I've been told. Got friends there too. I dare say he'll be back in a day or two. Why not put on one of your new skirts and that jacket and go down to the shop for me and fetch up a few groceries?'

So Emma went shopping, exchanging good mornings rather shyly with the various people she met. They were friendly, wanting to know if she liked the village and did she get on with the dogs? She guessed that there were other questions hovering on their tongues but they were too considerate to ask them.

Going back with her shopping, she reflected that, since she had promised to marry Paul, it might be a good thing to do so as soon as possible. He had told her to decide on a date. As soon after the banns had been read as could be arranged—which thought reminded her that she would certainly need something special to wear on her wedding-day.

Very soon, she promised herself, she would get the morning bus to Exeter and go to the boutique Paul had taken her to. She had plenty of money still—her own money too... Well, almost her own, she admitted, once the house was sold and she had paid him back what she owed him.

The time passed pleasantly, her head filled with the delightful problem of what she would wear next, and even the steady rain which began to fall as she walked on the moor with the dogs did nothing to dampen her spirits.

She got up early and took them out for a walk before her breakfast the next day and then, with Mrs Parfitt's anxious tut-tutting because she wouldn't get the taxi from the garage ringing in her ears, she got on the bus.

It was a slow journey to the city, since the bus stopped whenever passengers wished to get on or off, but she hardly noticed, and when it arrived at last she nipped smartly away, intent on her search for the perfect wedding-outfit.

Of course, she had had her dreams of tulle veils and elaborate wedding-dresses, but theirs wasn't going to be that sort of wedding. She should have something suitable but pretty, and, since she had an economical mind, something which could be worn again.

The sales lady in the boutique remembered her and nodded her head in satisfaction at the vast improvement in Emma's appearance now that she was wearing the tweed suit. The little hat she had persuaded her to buy had been just right... She smiled encouragingly. 'If I may say so, madam, that tweed is exactly the right colour for you. How can I help you?'

'I want something to wear at my wedding,' said Emma, and went delightfully pink.

The sales lady concealed a sentimental heart under her severely corseted black satin. She beamed a genuine smile. 'A quiet wedding? In church?'

Emma nodded. 'I thought a dress and jacket and a hat...'

'Exactly right, madam, and I have just the thing, if you will take a seat.'

Emma sat and a young girl came with the first of a selection of outfits. Very pretty, but blue would look cold in the church. And the next one? Pink, and with rather too many buttons and braid for her taste—it was too frivolous. The third one was the one—winter white in a fine soft woollen material, it had a short jacket and a plain white sheath of a dress.

'I'll try that one,' said Emma.

It fitted, but she had known that it would. Now that

she was wearing it she knew that it was exactly what she had wanted.

The sales lady circled her knowingly. 'Elegant and feminine. Madam has a very pretty figure.'

'I must find a hat...'

'No problem. These outfits for special occasions I always team up with several hats so that the outfit is complete.' She waved a hand at the girl, who opened drawers and tenderly lifted out a selection and offered them one by one.

Emma, studying her reflection, gave a sigh. 'I'm so plain,' she said in a resigned voice, and removed a confection of silk flowers and ribbon from her head.

The sales lady was good at her job. 'If I may say so, madam, you have fine eyes and a splendid complexion. Perhaps something... Ah, I have it.'

It looked nothing in her hand—white velvet with a pale blue cord twisted round it—but on Emma's head it became at once stylish, its small soft brim framing her face.

'Oh, yes,' said Emma, and then rather anxiously, 'I hope I have enough money with me.'

The older woman waved an airy hand. 'Please do not worry about that, madam. Any money outstanding you can send to me when you return home.'

Emma took off the hat and, while it and the outfit were being packed up, counted the money in her purse. There was more than enough when she was presented with the bill. She paid, feeling guilty at spending such a great deal of money. On the other hand she wanted to look her very best on her wedding-day. They would be happy, she promised herself, and stifled the sadness she felt that her mother wouldn't see her wed.

There were still one or two small items that she

needed. She had coffee and then bought them, and by that time she was hungry. She had soup and a roll in a small café tucked away behind the high street and then, since the bus didn't leave for another hour or so, wandered round the shops, admiring the contents of their windows, thinking with astonishment that, if she wanted, she could buy anything she desired, within reason. She would have plenty of money of her own when the house was sold; she would get Paul to invest it in something safe and use the interest. She need never ask him for a penny, she thought, and fell to wondering where he was and what he was doing.

Sir Paul, already on his way back from Edinburgh, had turned off the main road to pay a visit to his mother and father, and, as he always did, gave a smile of content as he took the Rolls between the gateposts and along the short drive which led to their home—an old manor-house built of Cotswold stone, mellow with age and surrounded by a large, rambling garden which even at the bleakest time of year looked charming.

One day it would be his, but not for many years yet he hoped, catching sight of his father pottering in one of the flowerbeds. He drew up before the door, got out and went to meet him and together they walked to the house, going in through the garden door. 'My dirty boots, Paul; your mother will turn on me if I go in through the front door.'

They both laughed. His mother, to the best of his knowledge, had never turned on anyone in her life. She came to meet them now. Of middle height, rather stout and with a sweet face framed by grey hair stylishly dressed, she looked delighted to see him.

'Paul—' she lifted her face for his kiss '—how

lovely to see you. Are you back at work again? Going somewhere or coming back?'

'Coming back. I can't stay, my dear, I need to get home—but may I come next weekend and bring the girl I'm going to marry to meet you both?'

'Marry? Paul—is it anyone we know?'

'No, I think not. She has lived at Buckfastleigh all her life except for her time at boarding-school. Her mother died recently. I hope—I think you will like her.'

'Pretty?' asked his mother.

'No—at least, she has a face you can talk to—peaceful—and she listens. Her eyes are lovely and she is also sensible and matter-of-fact.'

He didn't look like a man in love, reflected his mother. On the other hand, he was of an age to lose his heart for the rest of his life and beyond; she only hoped that she was the right girl. He had from time to time over the years brought girls to his parents' home and she hadn't liked any of them. They had all been as pretty as pictures, but he hadn't been in love with any of them.

'This is wonderful news, Paul, and we will make her very welcome. Come for lunch on Saturday. Can you stay until Monday morning?'

'I've a teaching round in the afternoon. If we leave soon after breakfast I can take Emma home first.'

'Emma—that's a pretty and old-fashioned name.'

He smiled. 'She's rather an old-fashioned girl.'

Watching him drive away presently, his mother said, 'Do you suppose it will be all right, Peter?'

'My dear, Paul is forty years old. He hasn't married sooner because he hadn't found the right girl. Now he has.'

Emma got off the bus in the village, walked the short distance to Paul's house, went along the alley and in through the side-door. Mrs Parfitt would be preparing dinner and she didn't want to disturb her. She went through to the hall and opened the drawing-room door, her parcels clamped under one arm.

Sir Paul was sitting by the fire, with the dogs resting their chins on his feet and Queenie on the arm of his chair. Emma gave a squeak of delight, dropped her parcels and hurried across the room.

'Paul! Oh, how lovely; you're home. Don't get up...'

He was already on his feet, his eyes very bright, scanning her happy face. He said lightly, 'Emma, you've been shopping again.' And she pulled up short beside him, conscious that she had been quite prepared to fling herself into his arms. The thought took her breath so that her voice didn't sound quite like hers.

'Well, yes, my wedding-dress.' She added earnestly, 'I couldn't buy it the other day because you mustn't see it until we're in the church.'

'A pleasure I look forward to.' He picked up the box and parcels she had dropped. 'You'd like a cup of tea? I'll tell Mrs Parfitt while you take off your things.'

When she came down the tea-tray was on a little table by the fire—tea in its silver teapot, muffins in their silver dish, tiny cakes.

She was pouring their second cups when he said quietly, 'Next Saturday we are going to my parents' home in the Cotswolds—just for the weekend.'

She almost dropped the pot. 'Oh, well, yes, of course. I—I hope they'll like me.' She put down the teapot carefully. 'I think that perhaps I'm not quite the kind of girl they would expect you to marry, if you see what I mean.'

'On the contrary. You will find that they will welcome

you as their daughter.' He spoke kindly but she could sense that it would be of no use arguing about it.

She said merely, 'That's good. I'll look forward to meeting them.'

'If you've finished your tea shall we go along to the vicarage and discuss dates with the vicar? If you're not too tired we can walk.'

The vicarage was on the other side of the church. I suppose I shall walk to my wedding, thought Emma as Paul rang the bell.

The vicar was a man of Paul's age. 'I'll read the first banns this Sunday, tomorrow, which means that you can marry any day after the third Sunday. You've a date in mind?'

They both looked at Emma, who said sensibly, 'Well, it will have to fit in with Paul's work, won't it?' She smiled at him. 'I know I'm supposed to choose, but I think you had better...'

'Will the Tuesday of the following week suit you? I believe I'm more or less free for a few days after that.' He glanced at Emma, who looked back serenely.

'In the morning?' she asked.

'Whenever you like; since I chose the day you must choose the time.'

She realised that she had no idea if there would be anyone else there, and her face betrayed the thought so plainly that Sir Paul said quickly, 'There will be a number of guests at the reception.'

He was rewarded by the look of relief on her face. 'Eleven o'clock,' she said.

The vicar's wife came in then, with a tray of coffee, and they sat for a while and talked and presently walked back to the cottage.

'You said there would be guests,' observed Emma, in a voice which held a hint of coolness.

'It quite slipped my mind,' he told her placidly. 'I'm sorry, Emma. We'll make a list this evening, shall we?' He smiled at her and she forgot about being cool. 'Mrs Parfitt will be in her element.'

The list was more lengthy than she had expected—his parents, his sisters and their husbands, a number of his colleagues from Exeter, friends from London, friends in and around the village, Doreen Hervey and her husband. 'And we must ask Mr Dobbs—I take it there is a Mrs Dobbs?'

'Yes, I think they'd like to come. Shall I write to them?'

'I'll get some cards printed—no time to have them engraved—and I'll phone everyone and tell them the cards will arrive later.' He glanced at his watch. 'I can reach several friends after dinner this evening.'

They told Mrs Parfitt the wedding-date when she came to wish them goodnight. 'The village will turn out to a man,' she told them happily. 'Been wanting to see you wed for a long time, sir. Your ma and pa will be coming, no doubt.'

'Indeed they are, Mrs Parfitt, and we hope you will be our guest too.'

'Well, now—that's a treat I'll enjoy. I'll need a new hat.'

'Then you must go to Exeter and get one. I'll drive you in whenever you wish to go.'

Emma saw very little of Paul until the weekend; he had consulting rooms in Exeter and saw his private patients there, and, in the evenings, although they discussed the wedding from time to time he made no mention of their future. All the guests were coming, he told her, and would she mind very much if he went to Exeter on the day after their wedding? He had promised to read a paper at a seminar; he had hoped to postpone it but it hadn't been possible.

'Well, of course you must go,' said Emma. 'May I come with you? I shan't understand a word but I'd very much like to be there.'

He had agreed very readily, but she wasn't sure if he was pleased about it or not.

They left early on Saturday morning and Emma sat silently beside him, hoping that she had brought the right clothes with her and that his parents would like her. She was then comforted by his quiet, 'Don't worry, Emma, everything will be all right.' And as though Willy and Kate had understood him, they had uttered gentle grumbling barks, and Willy had got down off the back seat and licked the back of her neck.

It was a day when spring had the upper hand and winter had withdrawn to the more remote stretches of the moor, and once they had bypassed Exeter and were racing up the motorway the country showed a great deal of green in the hedges. The car was blissfully warm and smelled of good leather, Paul's aftershave and the faint whiff of dog and, soothed by it, Emma decided in her sensible way that there was no point in worrying about something she knew very little about. So when Paul began a rambling conversation about nothing much she joined in quite cheerfully.

Just past Taunton he stopped for coffee and then turned off the motorway to drive across country—Midsomer Norton, Bath and then onwards towards Cirencester—to turn off presently into a country road which led them deep into the Cotswolds.

'Oh, this is nice,' said Emma. 'I like the houses—all that lovely pale yellow stone. Where are we exactly?'

'Cirencester is to the north-east, Tetbury is away to the right of us—the next village is where we are going.'

When he stopped the car in front of his parents' home, she sat for a moment, peering at it. 'It's beautiful,' she said softly. 'Do you love it very much?'

He said gravely, 'Yes, I do, and I hope that you will love it too. Come inside...' He took her by the elbow and went towards the opening door.

His mother stood there, smiling a welcome. She offered a cheek for his kiss and turned to Emma. 'Emma—such a pretty name—welcome, my dear.' She shook hands and then kissed Emma's cheek and tucked her arm in hers. 'Come and meet my husband.' She paused a moment to look up at her son. 'Paul, you described Emma exactly.'

He smiled but didn't speak, and when they entered the drawing-room and his father came to meet them he shook hands and then drew Emma towards him. 'Father, this is Emma—my father, Emma.'

Mr Wyatt wore his years lightly, and it was obvious where his son had got his good looks. She put out a hand and he took it and then kissed her. 'Welcome, my dear. We are delighted to have you here with us.'

After that everything was perfect. Going to bed that night in the charming bedroom, Emma reflected that she had had no need to worry—Paul's mother and father had been kindness itself, and Paul had taken her round the house and the large garden while Willy and Kate and his father's elderly spaniel trotted to and fro, dashing off following imaginary rabbits and then coming back to trot at their heels.

It had been an hour she didn't think she would forget;

they hadn't talked much but somehow there hadn't been the need for that. All the same, when they had gone back into the house for tea, she'd had the strange feeling that she knew Paul better than she had done.

In the evening, after dinner, they had sat talking about the wedding and who would be coming to it and Mrs Wyatt had admired her dress—one of the pretty ones Paul had persuaded her to have. 'You will make a charming bride,' she had told Emma. 'Paul is a lucky man.'

Emma, curling up in the comfortable bed, promised herself that she would make sure that he was. Not loving him didn't seem to matter, somehow, and she supposed that he felt the same about her. They were friends and they liked each other; everything would be all right, and on this cheerful thought she went to sleep.

They all went to church the next morning, and Emma got stared at. Somehow the news had got around that Sir Paul had got himself engaged at last and everyone wanted to see the bride-to-be. Wedged between father and son, Emma did her best not to notice the interested stares, hoping that they wouldn't be disappointed that she wasn't a girl whose good looks would match her bridegroom's. She peeped up at Paul's face and found him looking at her and took heart at his kind smile, knowing that he understood how she felt.

They left early on Monday morning, and his mother kissed her and gave her a little hug. 'My dear, we are so happy for you both. You are exactly right for Paul and we wish you every happiness. We shan't see you before your wedding-day—it's something we both look forward to. You'll meet the rest of the family then—they will love you, too.'

Emma got into the car feeling a pleasant glow of content; she had been accepted by Paul's family—something which mattered to her.

They were home by lunchtime but he went back to Exeter directly after, saying that he might be late back and that she wasn't to wait up for him. He didn't say why he was going and she didn't ask, although she longed to. Instead she offered to take the dogs for their walk in the late afternoon.

'Yes, do that. But not after teatime, Emma. I'll give them a good run when I get home.'

He patted her shoulder in what she considered to be a highly unsatisfactory manner and got back into the Rolls and drove away. The day, which had begun so pleasantly, had turned sour, and although she told herself that she had no reason to complain, she felt ill done by. She sat still when he had gone, looking at her ringless hand. Had he forgotten that it was the custom to give one's intended bride a ring? Or perhaps he thought that the unusual circumstances of their marriage didn't merit one.

Moping about and feeling sorry for herself would do no good, she told herself, and, leaving Queenie by the fire, she took Willy and Kate for a long walk.

She was late getting back to the cottage and Mrs Parfitt said severely, 'Another ten minutes and I'd have been getting worried about you, miss. Sir Paul said most particular that you weren't to go out after teatime. And quite right too!'

It was a remark which cheered her up a little, and tea round the fire, with the lamps lighted against the gloomy day, restored her usual good spirits. She spent a careful half-hour writing her bread-and-butter letter to Mrs Wyatt, then stamped it and left it on the hall table. The postman would take it in the morning.

She lingered over dinner, helped Mrs Parfitt clear the table and, since there was no sign of Paul, went to bed with a book. She read for a long time, one ear cocked for the sound of his footfall, but by midnight she was half-asleep. She put the book down, telling herself that this was no way to behave—there would probably be years of similar evenings, and if she lay in bed worrying about him she would grow old before her time. Queenie, glad at last that the bedside lamp was out, crept up beside her and she fell asleep.

When she went down to breakfast the next morning, Paul was already at the table. His good morning was cheerful and friendly. 'You slept well?' he wanted to know.

'Like a top, whatever that means! What a nice morning it is…'

'Yes, indeed—a pity I have to go back to Exeter this morning. Unfinished business, I'm afraid.'

'Would you like me to take the dogs out?' She buttered toast, not looking at him.

'I'll take them before I go; I'm sure you have a lot to do here.'

What, in heaven's name? Mrs Parfitt got upset if she offered to help in the house, the garden was beautifully kept by the part-time gardener, but there was a chance that she could go to the village shop for Mrs Parfitt…

'Oh, yes, I've lots to do,' she told him serenely.

'You won't mind if I leave you?' And at her cheerful, 'Of course not,' he got up.

On his way to the door, though, he paused and came back to the table. 'I must beg your forgiveness, Emma.' He took a small box from a pocket. 'I have been carrying this round since we left yesterday and forgot all about it.'

He took a ring out of the box and held it in the palm of his hand—sapphires and diamonds in an old-fashioned setting. 'It has been kept in the safe in father's study, waiting for the next bride in the family. It is very old and is handed down from one generation to the next.' He picked up her hand and slipped the ring on her finger.

'It fits,' said Emma.

'As I knew it would.' He bent and kissed her, a quick kiss which took her by surprise. 'That augers well for our future.'

Emma said, 'Thank you, Paul,' and, while she was still trying to think of something else to add to that, he patted her shoulder and was gone.

CHAPTER SIX

EMMA didn't see much of Paul during that week; he took her with him to Exeter one day, so that she might do some last-minute shopping, and once or twice he was home early so that they could walk the dogs together. On the Saturday he drove down to Buckfastleigh.

They had been invited by the Herveys to have drinks and at the same time they called at the house agent's. There were enquiries, they were told; it was certain that the house would sell, especially now that the warmer weather was coming.

'You don't mind waiting for the money?' asked Emma worriedly as they got back into the car.

'No, Emma, there's no hurry for that.' He turned to smile at her. 'There's time for us to get an armful of flowers and visit your mother's grave.'

She hadn't liked to ask but that was exactly what she wanted to do. He bought the flowers she chose—roses and carnations—and they took them to the quiet churchyard. Emma's sadness was mitigated by the feel of Paul's great arm round her shoulder and his unspoken sympathy.

The Herveys were delighted to see them and Emma was borne upstairs to see Bart, asleep in his cot. Emma was relieved to see that Nanny had been replaced by an older woman with a pleasant face and a ready smile.

'He's grown,' said Emma. 'He's perfect...'

'He's rather a duck,' said his mother fondly, 'and Nanny's splendid with him—and I'm getting better, aren't I, Nanny?'

On the way downstairs she took Emma's arm. 'Mike took one look at that other nanny and gave her notice,' she confided. 'Didn't fancy her at all—a regular sargeant major, he said she was. This one's an old dear, and she's taught me a lot—you know, how to hold Bart properly and what to do when he yells. I'm not afraid of him any more.'

She was quite serious; Emma murmured sympathetically, reflecting that it was fortunate that the Herveys could afford a nanny.

They had their drinks then, talking about the wedding and the baby and listening to Mike's amusing account of his trip to America. Then the two men went upstairs to see Bart and Mrs Hervey described in great detail what she intended to wear at the wedding.

Listening to her, Emma thought it likely that she would outshine the bride. Not that she minded—she liked Doreen Hervey; she might be helpless and unable to do much for herself but she was kind and friendly and light-hearted, and she went into raptures over Emma's ring.

'It's a family heirloom, isn't it? You deserve it, Emma, for you're such a nice girl, and Paul's the nicest man I know—excepting Mike, of course. He's frightfully rich, of course, and awfully important—but you'd never know, would you? Never says a word about himself—never told anyone why he was knighted... I don't suppose you would tell me? I'll not breathe a word...'

'Well, no,' said Emma. 'He wants to keep it a private matter.'

So private, she thought, that he had never mentioned it to her. She would ask him…

Which she did as they were driving back to Lustleigh, and was thwarted by his placid, 'Oh, you know how it is—names out of a hat and I happened to be lucky.' Even though he sounded placid there was something in his voice which prevented her from asking any more questions. Perhaps, she thought wistfully, when they had been married for a long time and had got to know each other really well he would tell her.

They went to church in the morning and heard their last banns read, and after the service an endless stream of people stopped to wish them well. They all wanted to know the date of the wedding.

'It will be very quiet—just family and a few close friends,' said Paul and, when pressed, told them the day on which they were to marry, knowing that if he didn't tell them they would find a reason to call at the cottage and ask Mrs Parfitt.

If Emma had hoped to see more of Paul during the next week she was disapointed; even at the weekend he was called away urgently to operate on a road casualty so that her wedding-day loomed without her having had the chance to get to know him better. Indeed, suspicion that he was avoiding her lurked at the back of her head and became so urgent that on the evening before her wedding, left to her own devices while he worked in his study, she put down the book she was reading, thumped on the door and then entered the study before she could change her mind.

He got up as she went in. 'Emma—what's wrong? You look as though…' He paused and asked mildly, 'Something has upset you?'

'Yes—no, I'm not sure.' She gave him a worried look. 'Why don't I see you more often? You're always going somewhere, and even when you're at home you keep out of my way. Don't you want to marry me? It's quite all right if you've changed your mind; it isn't as if... I wouldn't like you to get married to the wrong person and be unhappy.'

He came round the desk and took her hands in his. 'Emma, my dear girl, what can I say to reassure you? Only that I want to marry you and that you are the right person. If you haven't seen much of me it is because I've had a good deal of work, and I'm afraid that is something you will have to learn to live with.' He smiled down at her, a tender smile which set her heart thumping. 'And I haven't changed my mind, nor will that ever happen.'

'I've been silly,' said Emma. 'I'm sorry—and I've interrupted your work.'

He turned her round and put an arm round her shoulders. 'We will sit down and go over the arrangements for tomorrow.' He was propelling her gently out of the study and back into the drawing-room. 'Are you feeling nervous? No need—you know almost everyone who'll be there. The car will fetch you tomorrow morning; I know it's only a few yards to the church but I can't have my bride walking there...'

'The car? But what about you?'

'I'm spending the night at Eastrey Barton—the family are already there. It is considered very bad luck, so I'm told, for the bride and groom to spend the night before their wedding under the same roof. Mrs Parfitt will look after you and I'll phone you in the morning.'

'Oh, I thought we'd just have breakfast together as usual and then walk to church.'

'I have neglected you shamefully, Emma—the truth is'

'You forgot that you were getting married!' she finished for him, unaware that that hadn't been what he had been going to say.

She spoke matter-of-factly and Sir Paul gave a soundless sigh. Patience, he reminded himself—she wasn't ready to hear his reason for avoiding her company, and, when he was with her, treating her with a casual friendliness.

Dressed for her wedding, Emma took a final look at herself in the pier glass, and even to her critical eye she considered that she didn't look too bad. Not beautiful—brides were supposed to look beautiful—not even pretty, but the outfit suited her and the little hat framed her rather anxious face with its soft velvet brim.

She went downstairs to where Dr Treble, who was to give her away, waited, and was much heartened by his surprised admiration. He and Mrs Parfitt, who was on the point of leaving for the church, chorused their approval in no uncertain terms, so that she got into the car feeling more confident.

Her confidence faltered a little as they started down the aisle and she clutched the small bouquet of pink roses which Paul had given her in a nervous hand; she hadn't expected the church to be full of people—the entire village appeared to be in the pews, nodding and smiling at her as she passed them. When she reached the front pews Paul's mother looked round and smiled and nodded too, but Emma scarcely noticed her; her eyes were on Paul's broad back—if only he would turn round and look at her...

He did, smiling a little, and her heart gave a great

jump against her ribs so that she caught her breath. Her thoughts were wild; it was a bit late in the day to fall in love with him, wasn't it? And not at all a good idea either, for now everything was going to be a bit complicated.

She stood beside him and the vicar began to speak the opening words of the service. She did her best to listen but odd thoughts kept popping in and out of her head. She had loved him for quite a while, she thought, only she hadn't known it, and if she had would she have married him?

The solemn words the vicar was speaking cut across her reflections at last and she listened then. Never mind the future. She would make her vows and keep to them; she would be a good wife, and if Paul didn't need her love, only her companionship, then she would do her best to be the kind of person he wanted. When the moment came, she spoke her 'I will' in a clear, steady little voice that everyone could hear, and then took comfort from Paul's deep voice, as assured and certain as hers had been.

They exchanged rings then and went to sign the register, and presently were walking down the aisle and out into the bright morning, but before they could get into the Rolls they were surrounded by guests with cameras poised and had to pass through a barrage of confetti and good wishes.

Paul had been holding her hand, and as they reached the car at last gave it an encouraging squeeze. 'So much for our quiet wedding,' he said. 'I'm enjoying it, aren't you?'

'Oh, yes,' said Emma. 'It's the most wonderful day of my life.' She spoke with such fervour that he looked down at her, but the little hat shaded her face from his as she got into the car.

The rest of the day was like a dream; the cottage was full of people laughing and talking and drinking champagne and eating canapés. Paul had Emma by the hand, and as various friends greeted him he introduced her.

His sisters had been the first to join them after his mother and father—handsome young women who kissed her warmly and listened smilingly as their husbands flattered her gently and congratulated Paul—and after them there were people she realised she would meet again—colleagues from the hospital, several from London, old friends with their wives and of course the Herveys and Mr Dobbs and his wife.

Mr Dobbs had given her a smacking kiss. 'Wait till I tell 'em all about this,' he said. 'I'll make sure that Mrs Smith-Darcy gets the lot. I've taken some photos too.' He transferred his beaming smile to Sir Paul. 'You are a lucky man, and no mistake,' he told him.

Since they weren't going anywhere, the guests lingered, renewing acquaintances, plying Emma and Paul with invitations, and then at last taking their leave. The cake had been cut, the last toast drunk and Emma longed to take off her new shoes. The moment the last guest had gone, she did so. 'You don't mind, do you? Just for a few minutes—they're new...'

'And very pretty. You look charming, Emma, and I do like that hat.' He took her arm as they went indoors to where his mother and father and sisters were waiting. 'We're going out to dinner—just the family—but we can sit around for a while and talk.'

'I'll get Mrs Parfitt to make a pot of tea...'

'A splendid idea, although I suspect she's already got the kettle on.'

As indeed she had, and presently she bustled in with the tea-tray and a plate of cucumber sandwiches. 'After all that cake and bits and pieces,' she explained. 'Not but it wasn't a rare fine party.' Her eyes fell on the dogs, basking in the late afternoon sunshine. 'Queenie's in the kitchen having her tea.'

'And what about you, Mrs Parfitt?' asked Emma. 'You've worked so hard; you must have your tea too...'

'That I shall, ma'am—wetted it not five minutes ago with a nice boiled egg and a bit of toast.'

Emma, in bed that night, thought back over her wedding-day. It had ended on a light-hearted note at Eastrey Barton, where they had all dined splendidly with a great deal of talk and laughter, and she had been happy because Paul had given her a wedding-present—a double row of pearls which she had immediately worn.

When they had returned to the cottage he had kissed her goodnight—a quick, friendly kiss—almost a peck— she thought wistfully, but at least it was a kiss. It had been difficult not to kiss him back, but she hadn't. She would keep to her resolve of being a good companion, however hard it was, and perhaps in time he would come to love her. At least, she told herself stoutly, she had several advantages—she was his wife and she loved him.

The next day he took her to Exeter with him as he had promised, and she sat in the lecture hall and listened to him addressing a large and attentive audience. She understood very little of the lecture—that it was about bones went without saying, and some of it must have been amusing for the audience laughed quite often. When he had sat down they clapped for a long time before someone on the platform got up and made a speech about him in glowing terms.

Emma, sitting at the back of the hall, beamed with pride and Sir Paul, who had seen her the moment he started his lecture, smiled—his dear little Emma...

They had tea with a number of his colleagues—several foreign surgeons and members of the hospital board—and Emma—being Emma—had little to say for herself but listened to the opinions of various learned gentlemen who were quick to observe to Sir Paul that his wife was a charming young lady and a splendid listener. 'Such beautiful eyes,' sighed an Italian surgeon, over in England to exchange ideas with his colleagues. 'I hope we shall meet again.'

Driving back to Lustleigh presently, Paul repeated this. 'How fortunate that I'm not a jealous husband,' he said lightly. 'You were a great success, Emma.'

'Oh, was I? I didn't understand half of what they were talking about but they were all very nice to me.' She turned to look at him. 'Perhaps it was because I'm your wife and they were being polite.'

'No, no. They all fell for you...' He was laughing and that hurt.

'I expect it was my new clothes,' said Emma.

'You enjoyed the lecture?' he asked her.

'Very much, although I didn't understand very much of it. Do you lecture a great deal?'

'From time to time. Sometimes I'm invited to other countries—you shall come with me.'

'Oh, may I? Don't you have a secretary with you?'

'Yes, if it's a long tour, but for the present I shall be in England.'

'Not always at Exeter?'

'No—but I'm usually only away for a day or two—not long.'

At dinner that evening he asked her if she would like

to drive to Torquay in the morning. 'It's pleasant at this time of year—not too many people yet, and the dogs love the beach.'

She peeped at him over her glass. He looked tired and preoccupied—a carefree day by the sea would be pleasant. 'I'd love it,' she told him.

They left soon after breakfast, and since it was a clear day, Emma wore a skirt with a cashmere sweater and a velvet beret perched over one eye. 'Very fetching,' said Sir Paul. 'You are sure you'll be warm enough?'

He drove to the A38 and took the fork over Haldon to the coast and, as he had said, Torquay was not too crowded.

'Coffee first or walk the dogs?' he asked her.

'The dogs,' said Emma, conscious of two anxious, whiskery faces turned towards her. So they parked the car and took them down on to the beach and walked arm-in-arm for a mile or more, stopping every now and again to throw sticks for the dogs and look out to sea.

'It looks very cold,' said Emma, and then added, 'I expect you can swim...'

'Yes.' They were standing at the water's edge and he flung an arm around her shoulders. 'You don't?'

'Well, I tried—at school, you know—and once or twice when I went on holiday with Mother and Father. I think I'm a coward.'

His arm tightened. 'Nonsense. You haven't had the chance to learn, that's all. I'll teach you. I've a small yacht which I keep at Salcombe; we'll go there when I'm free.'

'I've never been on a yacht.'

'I shall very much enjoy having you for my crew,' he told her.

He took her to the Imperial Hotel for lunch—lobster bisque and *boeuf en croute*, rounded off by a chocolate soufflé, and washed down by a claret handled by the wine waiter as though it were a precious baby rather than a bottle.

Emma, who knew almost nothing about wines, took a sip, then another. 'It's perfect—I've never tasted anything as heavenly.'

Sir Paul thought it unlikely that she had, but he expressed the view that it was considered a good wine and that he was glad that she enjoyed it.

The day was fine. They walked again after lunch, on the beach once more but this time in the opposite direction, with the dogs rushing about, barking at the water, begging for sticks to be thrown. Presently they turned back and got into the car and began to drive back to Lustleigh, stopping on the way at a tea-room in one of the villages. It was old-fashioned—a front room in a thatched cottage—but they had a splendid tea of muffins, oozing butter, and a large pot of strong tea, while the dogs sat under the table, gobbling the bits of muffin Emma handed them.

'You'll spoil them,' observed Sir Paul.

She said at once, 'Oh, I'm sorry, I shouldn't have done it.'

He frowned, annoyed with himself for sounding as though he was criticising her. She saw the frown and guessed quite wrongly that he was vexed with her so that she became ill at ease.

The day had been heavenly—just being with him had been wonderful—but now, in her efforts to behave as the kind of wife he had wished for, she drew back from the friendly rapport they had had, still making small talk, but keeping him at arm's length while willingly answering him when he spoke.

He, however, was practised in the art of putting patients at their ease, and by the time they reached home she was her usual, friendly self and they dined together in the easy companionship that he was so careful to maintain.

That, she was to discover, was to be the last of their days together for some time, for he left directly after breakfast each morning and was rarely home before seven or eight o'clock in the evening. She hid her disappointment and showed a bright face when he got back—ready to listen about his day, even though she understood very little of what he had been doing. She was also careful not to chat at breakfast while he was glancing through his post. True, they had been out to dine on several evenings, but she saw little of him then, though it was pleasant to meet the people he counted his friends.

She filled her days with walking the dogs, working doggedly at a piece of tapestry she had begun with so much enthusiasm, not realising the amount of work and tiny stitches it required before it was finished. She was happy because she loved Paul, but she found herself counting the hours until he came home each evening.

They had been married for several weeks when he told her at breakfast that someone would deliver a Mini that morning. 'For you, Emma, so you can go wherever you want. I'll be home early today and you can take me for a drive in it.'

She smiled widely at him across the table. 'Paul, thank you—how perfectly splendid.' She added, 'I'll be very careful…'

He smiled. 'Keep to the roads around here until you're quite used to it. I'll be home before five o'clock so be ready for me.'

He dropped a kiss on her head as he went away.

The Mini, a nice shade of blue, arrived at lunchtime, and she got into it at once and drove to Bovey Tracey and back and then waited impatiently for Paul to come home. When he did she drove him to Moretonhampstead, very conscious of him sitting squashed up beside her.

'It's a bit small for you,' she said, driving carefully past the sheep wandering across the road.

'Indeed, but just right for you, I hope, Emma.'

'Yes, oh, yes. It's a wonderful present.'

Back home, as they sat at dinner he asked her, 'Do you find the days long, Emma?'

'Well, yes, a bit. You see, I've had to work all day for quite a time and I'm not really used to having so much leisure.'

'Would you like a little job? Voluntary, of course. There is a nursery at Moretonhampstead. It takes unwanted babies and toddlers—most of them are orphaned or abandoned. Not ill, but neglected and very underfed. Diana Pearson, who is in charge, is an old friend of mine and she tells me that she needs more help urgently. Would you like to go there once or twice a week and give a hand? No nursing, just common sense and a liking for infants.'

He wanted her to say yes, she was sure—perhaps that was why he had given her the car. She didn't hesitate. 'Yes, I'd love to help,' she told him.

'Good. We'll go there on Monday; I'm not operating until the afternoon. Would you ask Mrs Parfitt to have lunch ready for us at one o'clock? I'll bring you back and have lunch here.' He added, 'One or two days a week and not more than four hours at a time, Emma. It has to be interesting, not tiring and demanding, and never at the weekends.'

The nursery was on the outskirts of the town—a long, low building, with cheerfully coloured walls and a large playroom and several nurseries. Sir Paul walked in as though he knew the place well and went straight to a door with 'Office' written on it.

The young woman who got up as he went in was tall and dark with almost black eyes in a lovely face. She was elegantly dressed and she smiled at him in a way which gave Emma food for thought. Her greeting was casual enough and when Paul introduced her she shook hands with a pleasant murmur and another smile—quite different from the first one, though.

It was obvious that she knew all about Emma, for she said pleasantly, 'We'd love to have you here; we're desperate for help. Paul said two days in a week and not more than four hours at a time.' She put a hand on his arm and smiled at Emma, who smiled back, knowing that she was disliked just as she disliked the speaker. 'Come and look around—there are a lot of small babies at the moment. The travellers bring them in for a week or two's feeding up—the little ones get cold and quickly ill; it's not really an ideal life for babies, although the children seem happy enough.'

They went round the place together, and Emma said she would come each Tuesday and Thursday in the mornings. 'Is nine o'clock too early?'

'We take over from the night staff at eight o'clock, but that'll be too early for you.' Diana stole a look at Paul. 'Won't it, Paul?' She smiled as she spoke, and

Emma repressed a desire to slap her. If it hadn't been for Paul's obvious wish that she should have something to occupy her days she would have said there and then that she had changed her mind.

On the way back to the cottage Paul said carefully, 'You'll like Diana—she is a marvellous organiser. She has no need to work and it surprises me that she hasn't married—she's quite lovely, isn't she?'

'She's beautiful,' said Emma. 'Have you been friends for a long time?'

'Two or three years, I suppose. We met at a friend's house and found that we had a good deal in common.'

Emma kept her voice pleasant. 'Instant rapport—that's what it's called, isn't it? You meet someone and feel as though you've known them all your life...' She added before he could reply, 'I'm sure I shall enjoy giving a hand—thank you for thinking of it, Paul.'

'I wondered if you were becoming bored with life—I'm not at home much, am I?'

She said cheerfully, 'Well, I didn't expect you to be—doctors never are, are they?'

That evening he asked her if she would like to spend a weekend with his parents. 'Next weekend I'm free. We could drive up on Saturday afternoon and come back on the Sunday evening.'

'I'd like that.'

But first there was the nursery. She drove there in the Mini and within ten minutes, wrapped in a plastic pinny, she was bathing a very small baby in a room where five other babies were awaiting her attention.

Diana Pearson, elegant and beautiful, sitting behind her desk, had greeted her pleasantly but without warmth. 'Hello, Emma—so you have turned up. So many volunteer ladies change their minds at the last minute. Will you go to the end nursery and start bathings? Someone will be along to give you a hand presently.'

Emma had waited for more information but Diana had smiled vaguely and bent her head over the papers before her. At least she'd been credited with enough good sense to find her own way around, reflected Emma, and anyway she'd met another girl on the way to the nursery, who'd shown her where to find a pinny before hurrying off in the opposite direction.

Emma, not easily flurried, had found the pinny, assembled all that she needed to deal with the babies and picked up the first one...

She had just picked up the second baby, a small, wizened creature, bawling his head off, tiny fists balled in rage, eyes screwed up tightly, when she was joined by a middle-aged woman with a sour expression.

'New, are you?' she wanted to know as she tied her pinny. 'What's yer name?'

Not a local woman, thought Emma, and said pleasantly, 'Emma—Emma Wyatt, and yes, I'm new. I hope you'll tell me when I do something wrong.'

'You bet I will. 'Ere, you that Professor Wyatt's wife?'

'Yes, I am.'

'Well, don't expect me ter call yer 'yer ladyship', 'cos I'm not going to.'

'I'd like it if you'd call me Emma.'

The woman looked surprised. 'OK, I'm Maisie.' She picked up the third baby and began to take off its gown with surprisingly gentle hands. 'He's the worst of the bunch you've got there,' she observed. 'Proper little imp, 'e is—always shouting 'is 'ead off.'

Emma looked down at the scrap on her lap; he had

stopped crying and was glaring at her from bright blue eyes. 'He's rather sweet…'

Maisie gave a cackle of laughter. 'Your first day, isn't it? Wait till you've been 'ere a couple of months—that's if you last as long as that.'

'Why do you say that?'

'You'll find out for yerself—Madam there, sitting in her office, doing nothin'—that is, until someone comes along. Pulls the wool nicely over their eyes, that she does. That 'usband of yours—she's 'ad her sights on 'im this last year or more. 'Ad her nose put out of joint and no mistake.' She was pinning a nappy with an expertise Emma envied. 'Better watch out, you 'ad.'

The baby, freshly bathed and gowned, looked up at Emma with interest; she picked him up and tucked his small head under her chin and cuddled him.

''Ere, there ain't no time for cuddling—leastways not in the mornings—there's the feeds to do next.'

So Emma put him back in his cot and set to work on the fourth baby, a placid girl who blew bubbles and waved her small arms at her. Maisie had finished before her; she was already feeding the first baby by the time Emma had tidied everything away and fetched her three bottles from the little pantry.

When the infants had been fed and lay sleeping it off, she and Maisie had to tidy the nursery, put everything ready for the afternoon and then go and have their coffee. They sat together in the small room set aside for them and Emma listened to Maisie's numerous tips about the work.

'Have you been here long?' she asked.

'Upwards of two years. It's a job, see. Me old man scarpered off and the kids are at school all day—keeps me mind off things.'

She blew on her coffee and took a gulp. 'You going ter stick it out? It's not everyone's cup of tea.'

'Well, I like babies,' said Emma, 'and my husband's away almost all day. He told me that Miss Pearson was short-handed and asked if I'd like to help out, so I'll stay for as long as I'm needed. I only come twice a week.'

Maisie eyed her thoughtfully over her mug. 'Persuaded 'im, she did? Men—blind as bats! Never mind the "lady this" and "lady that"—you're a nice young woman, so keep those eyes of yours peeled.'

'Thank you for your advice. Shall I see you on Thursday?'

'Yep. Me, I come every morning—oftener if it gets really busy. Some of the babies will be going back to their mums tomorrow—bin waiting for an 'ouse or flat or whatever, yer see.'

'I hope the same babies will be here when I come on Thursday.'

'Well, Charlie—that's the little 'owler—e'll be with us for a while yet. 'Is mum's in prison for a couple of months—won't 'ave 'im near 'er.'

'Why ever not?'

'Dunno; bit flighty, I dare say.' She put down her mug. 'We gotta bag the wash before we go.'

Diana came out of the office as Emma took off her pinny. 'Going? See you on Thursday and many thanks. Oh, would you ask Paul to call in some time? I need his advice about one of the toddlers—a congenital dislocation of the hip—I think the splint needs adjusting.'

'I'll tell him,' said Emma. 'I'm sure he'll come when he has the time.'

Diana laughed. 'He usually comes whenever I ask him to, whether he's busy or not—we're old friends.'

Emma dredged up a smile. 'That's nice—I'll see you on Thursday.'

She drove back home, ate the lunch Mrs Parfitt had ready for her and then took the dogs for a long walk. She had a great deal to think about.

'It's a good thing I'm married to him,' she told Willy, who was loitering beside her. 'I mean, it's an advantage, if you see what I mean—and I love him. The point is, does he love her? That's something I have to find out. But if he does why did he marry me?' She stopped and Kate came lumbering back to see why. 'If it was out of pity...?' She sounded so fierce that Willy gave a whimper.

Paul was home for tea, which surprised her. 'How nice,' she said, and beamed at him. 'Have you had a busy day?'

'I've beds at the children's hospital and an outpatients clinic at Honiton; I seem to have spent a lot of my time driving from here to there.' He bit into one of Mrs Parfitt's scones. 'Tell me, did you enjoy your morning?'

'Very much. I bathed three babies and fed them. There was someone else there in the nursery—a nice woman who was very friendly and helpful. Oh, and Diana says could you go and see the baby with the dislocated hip? She thinks the splint needs changing.'

'It'll have to be tomorrow evening. I've a list in the morning and a ward-round in the afternoon and a couple of private patients to see after that.'

'Where do you see them?'

'I've rooms in Southernhay. I'll phone Diana presently and tell her when I'll be free.'

'I'll ask Mrs Parfitt to make dinner a bit later, shall I?'

'Yes, do that if you will. Did you take the dogs out?'

'Yes, it was lovely on the moor. After all it is summer.'

'That doesn't mean to say we shan't get some shockingly bad weather.' He got up. 'I've some phoning to do, then I'll take the dogs for ten minutes.' He smiled at her. 'You must tell me more about the nursery when I get back.'

The following evening he phoned at teatime to say that he would be home later than he had expected and that she wasn't to wait dinner for him. 'I'll get something here,' he told her.

She gave him a cheerful answer and spent the rest of the evening imagining him and Diana dining together at some quiet restaurant. She knew it was silly to do so but she seemed unable to think of anything else.

Perhaps it wasn't so silly either, she told herself, lying in bed later, waiting for the sound of the car and dropping off to sleep at last without having heard it.

He was already at the table when she went down to breakfast. He wished her good morning. 'You don't mind if I get on? I've a busy day ahead.'

'Did you have a busy time last night?' She kept her voice casually interested.

'Yes. I trust I didn't disturb you when I got back?'

'Will you go and see the baby today? Do you want me to give Diana a message?'

He gave her a thoughtful look. 'No need. I saw her yesterday.'

'Oh, good,' said Emma, bashing her boiled egg, wishing it was Diana.

CHAPTER SEVEN

DIANA'S greeting when Emma reached the nursery was friendly. It was as though she was trying to erase her rather cool manner towards her; she asked if she was quite happy with the babies, if she would like to alter her hours and expressed the hope that she wasn't too tired at the end of her morning's work. Emma took all this with a pinch of salt, not convinced by all this charm that Diana was going to like her—and, anyway, she didn't like Diana.

It was refreshing, after all that sweetness, to listen to Maisie's down-to-earth talk, which covered everything under the sun—the royal family, the government, the price of fish and chips and the goings-on of the young couple who had rented rooms beneath hers—and all the while she talked she attended to the babies, raising her voice above their small cries.

They had finished the bathing and were feeding them when she said, 'Your old man was 'ere yesterday—late too.'

Emma was feeding Charlie, who was content for once, sucking at his bottle as though it would be torn from him at any moment. 'Yes, I know,' she said quietly.

Maisie turned her head to look at her. 'You're a quiet one, but I bet me last penny you'll get the better of 'er.'

'Yes, I believe I shall,' said Emma, and smiled down at Charlie's small face. He wasn't a pretty baby—he was too pale and thin for that. It was to be hoped that when his mother claimed him once more—if she ever did—he'd look more like a baby and not a cross old man. She kissed the top of his head and gave him a quick cuddle and then put him over her shoulder so that he could bring up his wind.

It was after they had had dinner together that evening that Paul told her that he was going to Boston in two days' time.

Emma said, 'Boston? You mean Boston, USA?'

'Yes, and then on to New York, Philadelphia and Chicago. I shall be away for ten days, perhaps a little longer.' He said, carefully casual, 'I expect the trip would be a bit boring for you.'

She was quick to decide that he didn't want her with him. 'Yes, I think it might be,' she said. 'Will you be lecturing?'

She looked to see if he was disappointed but his face gave nothing away. 'If you need help of any sort, phone John Taggart, my solicitor; he'll sort things out for you. I've opened an account for you at my bank—I have also arranged for a joint account but I'd like you to have your own money. The house agent phoned to say that he has a possible buyer for your house; send everything to John—he'll deal with it.'

'The dogs will miss you,' said Emma. She would miss him too, but she wasn't going to tell him that. 'There's a card from the Frobishers—they've asked us to dinner. I'll write and explain, shall I?'

'Yes, do that. Suggest we take up their invitation when I get back.'

It was all very business-like and she did her best to match her manner to his. 'Shall I write to your mother and tell her that we shan't be coming for the weekend?'

'I phoned her last night. They are very sorry not to be seeing us.'

'I could drive myself...'

'I'd prefer you not to, Emma.'

The cottage seemed very quiet when he had gone. Emma couldn't bear to be in it and took the dogs for a long walk on the moor; they walked for miles and the austere vastness of it made his absence bearable. 'It's only for just over a week,' she told the dogs. 'But how shall I bear to be away from him for so long?'

A problem solved for her by Diana, who, when Emma went on Tuesday as usual, asked her if she could manage to help out for a third morning.

'We're so short of staff, I don't know which way to turn. I'm so glad that Paul didn't want you to go with him.' She laughed gently. 'Wives can be a bit of an encumbrance sometimes. It was so wise of him to marry someone like you, Emma.'

Emma asked why.

'Well, you're not demanding, are you? You're content to sit at home and wait for him to come back—just what he needed...'

Emma said, 'Yes, I think it is. He leads a busy life.'

Diana laughed again. 'Yes, but he always has time for his friends. He and I have such a lot in common.'

'I expect you have,' said Emma sweetly, 'but not marriage.' Her smile was as sweet as her voice. 'I'll get started on the babies,' she said.

Maisie, already at work with her three, looked up as she went into the nursery. ''Ello, Emma, what's riled you? 'As her 'igh and mightiness been tearing yer off a strip?'

'No—just a slight difference of opinion. I'm going to do an extra morning, Maisie; I hope you'll be here too.'

'Come every day, don't I, love? I'll be here. So'll Charlie there, from wot I 'eard. 'Is mum don't really want 'im, poor little beggar.'

'What will happen to him?' Emma was lifting him from his cot; he was bawling as usual.

'Foster-mum if they can find one, or an orphanage...'

'He's so small...'

'Plenty more like 'im,' said Maisie. 'Maybe there'll be someone who don't mind a bad-tempered kid.'

'Well, I'd be bad-tempered if I were he,' said Emma, smiling down at the cross little face on her lap. 'Who's a lovely boy, then?' she said.

She thought of Paul constantly, and when he phoned from Boston that night she went around in a cloud of content which was, however, quickly dispelled when she went into the nursery the next day.

'Heard from Paul?' asked Diana, with a friendly concern Emma didn't trust.

'Well, yes. He phoned yesterday evening...'

'He always does.' Diana smiled at Emma—a small secret smile, suggesting that words weren't necessary.

She had no right to be jealous, reflected Emma, bathing a belligerent Charlie, for she had no hold on Paul's feelings, had she? He had wanted a companion and the kind of wife to suit his lifestyle. He had never promised love...

That afternoon when she took the dogs on to the moor she saw the clouds piling up over the tors and felt the iciness of the wind. Bad weather was on the way, and even though it was summer the moor could be bleak and cold. She turned for home and was thankful for the bright fire in the drawing-room and the delicious tea Mrs Parfitt had ready for her.

Diana came out of her office as she arrived at the nursery on Thursday. 'Emma, I'm so glad to see you. You know the moor well, don't you? There's a party of travellers camping somewhere near Fernworthy Reservoir—one of them phoned me. We've one of their toddlers here already and he says there are several children sick—not ill enough for the doctor—colds, he thinks, and perhaps flu. He asked me to send someone with blankets, baby food and cough medicine. I wonder if you would go? It's not far but a bit out of the way. Perhaps you can get them to come off the moor until the weather gets warmer again.'

'Yes, of course I'll go. I'll phone Mrs Parfitt, though, so that she can take the dogs out if I'm not back.'

Mrs Parfitt didn't fancy the idea at all. 'Sir Paul would never allow it,' she demurred. 'You going off on your own like that.'

'I'll be gone for an hour or two,' said Emma. 'It's not far away, you know...'

Mrs Parfitt snorted. 'Maybe not, madam, but it's so isolated it could be the North Pole.'

It wasn't quite the North Pole but it was certainly isolated. Emma had a job finding the camp, tucked away from the narrow road which led to nowhere but the reservoir. When she found it eventually it took quite a time to unload the blankets and baby food and hand them over.

There were half a dozen broken-down buses and vans drawn up in a semicircle and their owners clamoured for her attention as she was led from one to another ramshackle vehicle. In one of them she found a sick baby—

too ill to cry. 'She's ill,' she told the young woman who was with her. 'She needs medical attention—will you bring her to the nursery? I'll take you now...'

The girl needed a lot of persuading. ''Tis only a cold,' she told Emma. 'There's half a dozen kids as bad. Come in and look if you don't believe me.'

She was right. There were more than half a dozen, though—some of them small babies. Emma, although no nurse, could recognise the signs of whooping cough when she saw it. It would need several ambulances to take them to the nursery. 'Look,' she said to one of the older women, 'I haven't room to take them all, but I'll go back now and send an ambulance for them.'

They gathered round her, all talking at once, but at last she got back into the Mini, with the baby and its mother in the back, and began her journey back to Moretonhampstead. As Diana had said, it wasn't far, but the road was narrow and winding and little used and there were no houses or farms in sight. She was glad when the reached the nursery and she could hand the baby and mother over to Diana.

It was Maisie who led them away while Emma explained to Diana that there were more babies and toddlers needing help. 'An ambulance?' she suggested. 'They are really quite ill and it's so cold for them.'

Diana frowned. 'Wait here. I'll see if I can get help. Go and have a cup of coffee; you must need one.'

When Emma returned Diana shook her head. 'Would you believe it, there's nothing to be had until tomorrow morning—it's not urgent you see...'

'But they need more baby food and someone to clean them up—nappies and warm clothes.'

Diana appeared to think. 'Look, I wouldn't ask it of everyone but you're so sensible, Emma. If I get more stuff packed up would you take it back? Why not go back to Lustleigh and pack an overnight bag just in case you feel you can't leave them? I'll get a doctor to them as soon as I can and you can go straight home once he's got organised.'

'You're sure there's no one available?'

'Quite sure. There's a flap on with a major road accident—whooping cough just doesn't count.'

Emma was only half listening, which was a pity for then she might have queried that, but she was worried about the babies wheezing and gasping, so far from the care they needed. She said, 'All right, I'll go. I wish Paul were here...'

'Oh, my dear, so do I. He's such a tower of strength—we have been so close.' Diana's voice was soft and sad. 'We still are and I know you won't mind; it isn't as if you love each other.' She turned away and dabbed at a dry eye. 'You see, his work is all-important to him; he cannot afford to be distracted by the all-embracing love I—' She choked and took a long breath. 'Of course, he has explained all that to you—he told me how understanding you were.'

Emma said, 'I'd better be on my way,' and left without another word.

She went over the conversation word for word as she drove back to the cottage, and although she hated Diana she had to admit that it was all probably true. Paul didn't love her; he liked her enough to marry her, though, knowing that she would provide the calm background his arduous work demanded, whereas Diana's flamboyant nature would have distracted him.

It was well into the afternoon by now, and the sky was threatening rain. She hurried into the cottage, explained to Mrs Parfitt that she might not get back that night and ran upstairs to push essentials into a shoulder-bag. Mrs Parfitt came after her. 'You didn't ought to go,' she said worriedly. 'Whatever will Sir Paul say when he hears?'

'Well, he doesn't need to know. I'm only going to the reservoir, and don't worry, Mrs Parfitt, there'll be a doctor there tomorrow and I'll come home.' She turned to look at the faithful creature. 'Think of those babies—they really need some help.'

'Sir Paul wouldn't let you go, ma'am, but since you won't listen to me at least you'll have a bowl of soup and a nice strong cup of tea.'

Emma, who hadn't had her lunch, agreed, wolfed down the soup and some of Mrs Parfitt's home-made bread, drank several cups of tea and got back into the car. It was raining now and the wind had got up. She waved goodbye to Mrs Parfitt and Willy and Kate and drove back to the nursery.

It was amazing how much could be packed into the Mini; it was amazing too how helpful Diana was. 'Don't worry,' she told Emma. 'Someone will be with you just as soon as possible.'

She waved goodbye as Emma drove away, then went into the office and picked up the phone. 'There's no hurry to send anyone out to that camp on the moor. I've sent everything they need and the girl who is taking the stuff is sensible and capable. I'll let you know more in the morning!'

Emma was still a mile or so from the reservoir when she saw the first wisps of mist creeping towards her, and five minutes later she was in the thick of it. It was eddying to and fro so that for a moment she could see ahead and then the next was completely enshrouded.

She had been caught in the moorland mists before

now; to a stranger they were frightening but she had learnt to take them in her stride. All the same, she was relieved when she saw the rough track leading to the camp and bumped her way along it until the first of the buses loomed out of the mist. The mist had brought Stygian gloom with it and she was glad to see the lights shining from the open doorways. As she got out several of the campers came to surround her.

They were friendly—happy in the way they lived, making nothing of its drawbacks—but now they were anxious about the babies and Emma, taken to see them, was anxious too. No expert, she could still see that they were as ill as the one she had taken to the nursery. She handed out the blankets, baby food and bags of nappies, drank the mug of strong tea she was offered and prepared to return.

The mist had thickened by now and it was almost dark—to find her way wouldn't be easy or particularly safe; she would have to stay where she was until the morning and, since there were hours to get through, she could curl up in the back of the Mini for the night. She helped with the babies, looking at their small white faces and listening to their harsh breathing and hoping that, despite the awful weather, an ambulance or at least a doctor would come to their aid.

No one came, however, so she shared supper with one of the families and, after a last worried look at the babies, wrapped herself in a blanket and curled up on the Mini's back seat. It was a tight fit and she was cold, and the thin wails of the babies prevented her from sleeping, and when she at last lightly dozed off she was awakened almost immediately by one of the men with a mug of tea.

The mist had lifted. She scrambled up, tidied herself

as best she could and got back into the car. If she drove round the reservoir and took the lane on the other side she would reach a hamlet, isolated but surely with a telephone. She explained what she was going to do and set off into the cold, bleak morning.

It was beginning to rain and there was a strong wind blowing; summer, for the moment, was absent. The lane was rutted and thick with mud and there was no question of hurrying. She saw with relief a couple of houses ahead of her and then a good-sized farm.

There was a phone. The farmer, already up, took her into the farmhouse when she explained, and shook his head. 'They'm foolish folk,' he observed. 'Only just there, I reckon. Leastways they weren't there when I was checking the sheep a few days ago.' He was a kindly man. 'Reckon you'd enjoy a cuppa?'

'Oh, I'd love one, but if I might phone first? The babies do need to go into care as quickly as possible.'

A cheerful West Country voice answered her. They'd be there right away, she was told, just let her sit tight till they came. Much relieved, she drank her tea, thanked the farmer and drove back to tell the travellers that help was on the way.

'Likely they'll move us on,' said one woman.

'It's common land, isn't it? I dare say they'll let you stay as long as the babies are taken care of. I expect they'll take them to hospital and transfer them to the nursery until they are well again. You'll be able to see them whenever you all want to. Some of you may want to go with them.' She looked around her. 'I can give three of you lifts, if you like.'

One of the younger women offered to go.

'How ever will you get back?' asked Emma.

'Thumb a lift and walk the last bit—no problem.'

The ambulance came then, and Emma stood aside while the paramedics took over. They lifted the babies into the ambulance presently, offered the young woman who was to have gone with Emma a seat, and drove away. That left her free to go at last. No one wanted a lift—they were content to wait and see what the young woman would tell them when she got back. Emma got into her car and drove home, to be met at the door by an agitated Mrs Parfitt.

'You're fit to drop,' she scolded kindly. 'In you come, madam, and straight into a nice, hot bath while I get your breakfast. Like as not you've caught your death of cold.'

Not quite death, as it turned out, but for the moment she was very tired and shivery. The bath was bliss, and so were breakfast and the warm bed she got into afterwards.

'I must ring the nursery,' she said worriedly, and began to get out of bed again, to Queenie's annoyance.

'I'll do that,' said Mrs Parfitt. 'No good going there for a day or two, and so I'll tell that Miss Pearson.'

'I'm not ill,' said Emma peevishly, and fell asleep.

She woke hours later with a head stuffed with cotton wool and a sore thorat and crept downstairs, to be instantly shooed back to her bed by Mrs Parfitt bearing hot lemon and some paracetamol.

'It's more than my job's worth, Lady Wyatt, to let you get up. Sir Paul would send me packing.'

Emma, aware that Mrs Parfitt only called her Lady Wyatt when she was severely put out, meekly got back into bed.

'Did you phone the nursery?' she croaked.

'I did, and there is no need for you to go in until you are free of your cold. You'd only give it to the babies.'

Mrs Parfitt eyed her anxiously. 'I wonder if I should get the doctor to you, ma'am?'

'No, no—it's only a cold; I'll be fine in a day or two.'

Sir Paul, back from his travels, drove himself straight to the hospital, listened impatiently to his senior registrar's litany of things which had gone wrong during his absence and then, eager to get back home, phoned his secretary, who read out a formidable list of patients waiting for his services.

'Give me a day?' he begged her. 'I've a short list on the day after tomorrow. I'll come to my rooms in the afternoon—I leave it to you...'

He was about to ring off when she stopped him. 'Sir Paul, Miss Pearson phoned several times, and said it was most urgent that she should see you as soon as you got back.'

He frowned. 'Why didn't she speak to my registrar?'

'I don't know, sir; she sounded upset.'

'I'll call in on my way home.'

He was tired; he wanted to go home and see Emma, watch her face light up when she saw him. She might not love him but she was always happy to be with him. He smiled as he got out of the car and went along to Diana's office.

He might be tired but good manners necessitated his cheerful greeting. 'You wanted to see me; is it very urgent? I'm now on my way home.'

'I had to see you first,' said Diana. She was, for her, very quiet and serious. 'It's about Emma. Oh, don't worry, she's not ill, but I'm so upset. You see, she went dashing off; she simply wouldn't listen...'

Sir Paul sat down. 'Start at the beginning,' he said quietly.

Which was just what Diana had hoped he would say. She began to tell him her version of what had happened and, because she was a clever young woman, it all sounded true.

Sir Paul let himself into his house quietly, took off his coat and, since there were no lights on in the drawing-room, went to the little sitting-room at the back of the house. Emma was there, with Queenie on her lap and the dogs draped over her feet.

When he walked in she turned round, saw who it was, flew to her feet and ran across to him in a flurry of animals. 'Paul—you're back!' Her voice was still hoarse, and her nose pink from constant blowing, and it was a silly thing to say but she couldn't hide her delight.

He closed the door behind him and stood leaning against it, and it was only then that she realised that he was in a rage. His mouth was a thin hard line and his eyes were cold.

'What possessed you to behave in such a foolish manner?' he wanted to know. 'Why all the melodrama? What are the ambulances for? Or the police, for that matter? What in the name of heaven possessed you, Emma? To go racing off on to the moor in bad weather, sending dramatic messages, spending the night in a God-forsaken camp. Ignoring Diana's pleading to wait and give her time to phone for help. No, you must race away like a heroine in a novel, bent on self-glory.'

Emma said in a shaky voice, 'But Diana—'

'Diana is worth a dozen of you.'

It was a remark which stopped her from uttering another word.

'We'll talk later,' said Sir Paul, and went away to his study and sat down behind his desk, his dogs at his feet.

He'd been too hard on her; he tried not to think of her white, puzzled face with its pink nose, but he had been full of rage, thinking of all those things which could have happened to her. 'The little idiot,' he told the dogs. 'I could wring her darling neck.'

Emma gave herself ten minutes to stop shaking, then went in search of Mrs Parfitt. 'Sir Paul's home,' she told her. 'Can we stretch dinner for three?'

Mrs Parfitt gave her a thoughtful look, but all she said was, 'I'll grill some more cutlets and shall I serve a soup first? No doubt he's hungry after that journey.'

'That would be fine, Mrs Parfitt. I dare say he's famished. Could we have dinner quite soon?'

'Half an hour, ma'am—gives him time to have a drink and stretch out in his study.'

Emma went to her room, re-did her face and pinned her hair back rather more severely than usual, and then practised a few expressions in the looking-glass—a look of interest, a cool aloofness—she liked that one best...

Downstairs again, in the drawing-room, she picked up her tapestry work and began poking the needle in and out in a careless fashion, practising cool aloofness. She succeeded so well that when Paul came into the room intent on making his peace with her he changed his mind at once—the look she cast him was as effective as a barbed wire fence.

All the same, after a moment or two he essayed some kind of a conversation while he wondered how best to get back on a friendly footing once more.

Emma, her hurt and anger almost a physical pain, had no intention of allowing him to do that. She sat, mangling her needlework most dreadfully, silent except when it was asolutely necessary to say yes or no.

They had their dinner in silence, and as they got up

from the table Paul said, 'I think we should have a talk, Emma.'

She paused on her way to the door. 'No, I have understood you very well, Paul; there is no need to say it all over again.'

'Do I take it that you don't wish to work at the nursery any more?'

Her eyes were very large in her pale face. 'I shall go tomorrow morning as usual. Why not?'

His cold, 'Just as you wish,' was as icy as her own manner.

At breakfast she treated him with a frigid politeness which infuriated him—asking him if he would be late home, reminding him that they were due to attend a dinner party on the following evening and wishing him a cool goodbye as he got up to go.

When he had gone she allowed her rigid mouth to droop. She supposed that in a while they would return to their easy-going relationship, but it wouldn't be the same—he had believed Diana, he had mocked her attempts at helping the travellers and, worst of all, he hadn't asked her if any of the things Diana had told him were true. So, if his opinion of her was so low why had he married her? To provide a screen of respectability so that he and Diana could continue as they were? So why hadn't he married her?

Emma's thoughts swirled around in her tired head and didn't make sense. All she did know was that Diana had lied about her and Paul had listened willingly. She didn't think that Diana would expect her back but she was going. Moreover, she would behave as though nothing unusual had occurred, only now she would be on her guard. It was a pity that she had fallen in love with Paul but, since she had, there was nothing more she could do about it—only make sure that Diana didn't get him.

Her imagination working overtime, Emma took herself off to the clinic.

It was a source of satisfaction actually to see that Diana was actually surprised and a little uncomfortable when she walked in.

'Emma—I didn't expect you. You're sure you feel up to it? I heard that you had a heavy cold.'

'Not as heavy as all that. I'll wear a mask, shall I? Are there any new babies?'

Diana's eyes slid away from hers. 'Three from that camp. They're in isolation—whooping cough. They were in a pretty poor way, you know.' She added casually, 'I hear that Paul is back?'

'Yes, didn't he come to see you? I thought he might have popped in on his way home. He's got a busy day— I dare say he'll do his best to call in this evening. I'd better get on with the bathings or I'll have Maisie on my tail.'

Maisie was already busy with the first of her three babies. She looked up as Emma wrapped her pinny round her and got everything ready before picking up Charlie, who was bawling as he always did.

'I heard a lot,' said Maisie. 'Most of which I don't believe. You look like something the cat's dragged in.'

'As bad as that? And I don't think you need to believe any of it, Maisie.'

'You're a right plucky un coming back 'ere. I couldn't 'elp but 'ear wot madam was saying—being busy outside the office door as it were. And that 'usband of yours coming out like a bullet from a gun, ready to do murder. If 'e'd been a bit calmer I'd 'ave spoke up. But 'e almost knocks me over, sets me back on me feet and all without a word. 'E's got a nasty temper and no mistake.'

They sat in silence for a few minutes, then Maisie asked, 'Going to tell 'er awf, are yer?' She scowled. 'I could tell a few tales about 'er if you don't.'

'No—please, Maisie, don't do that. There's a reason…'

'Oh, yeah? Well, yer knows best, but if yer want any 'elp you just ask old Maisie.'

'I certainly will, and thank you, Maisie. I can't explain but I have to wait and see…'

'You're worth a dozen of 'er,' said Maisie, which brought a great knot of tears into Emma's throat, so that she had to bury her face in the back of Charlie's small neck until she had swallowed them back where they belonged.

Sir Paul came home late that evening and Emma, beyond asking politely if he had had a busy day, forbore from wanting to know where he had been. Anyway, Maisie, who was at the nursery for most of the day, would tell her soon enough if he had been to see Diana.

They exchanged polite remarks during dinner and then he went to his study, only coming to the drawing-room as she was folding away her tapestry. Sir Paul, a man of moral and physical courage, quailed under her stony glance and frosty goodnight.

Where, he asked himself, was his enchanting little Emma, so anxious to please, always so friendly and so unaware of his love? He had behaved badly towards her, but couldn't she understand that it was because he had been so appalled at the idea of her going off on her own like that? Perhaps Diana had exaggerated a little; he would go and see her again.

*   *   *

Emma wasn't going to the nursery the following morning. She took the dogs for a long walk and spent an agreeable half-hour deciding which dress she would wear to the dinner party. It was to be rather a grand affair, at one of the lovely old manor-houses on the outskirts of the village, and she wanted to make a good impression.

She had decided to wear the silver-grey dress with the long sleeves and modest neckline, deceptively simple but making the most of her charming shape. She would wear the pearls too, and do her hair in the coil the hairdresser had shown her how to manage on her own.

She had changed and was waiting rather anxiously for Paul to come home by the time he opened the door. She bade him good evening, warned him that he had less than half an hour in which to shower and change, and offered him tea.

He had taken off his coat and was standing in the doorway. 'Emma—I went to the camp this afternoon—'

She cut him short gently. 'You must tell me about it—but not now, you haven't time...'

He didn't move. 'I went to see Diana too.'

'Well, yes, I quite understand about that, but I don't want to talk about it, if you don't mind.' She added in a wifely voice, 'We're going to be late.'

He turned away and went upstairs and presently came down again, immaculate in his dinner-jacket, his face impassive, and courteously attentive to her needs. They left the cottage, got into the car and drove the few miles to the party.

It was a pleasant evening; Emma knew several of the people there and, seated between two elderly gentlemen bent on flattering her, she began to enjoy herself. Paul, watching her from the other end of the table, thought how pretty she had grown in the last few weeks. When they got home he would ask her about her night in the camp.

The men and women he had talked to there had been loud in her praise.

'Saved the kids lives,' one young man had said. 'Acted prompt, she did—and gave an 'and with cleaning 'em up too. Didn't turn a hair—took our little un and 'er mum back with 'er and then came back in that perishing fog—couldn't see yer 'and in front of yer face. Proper little lady, she were.'

He bent his handsome head to listen to what his dinner partner was talking about—something to do with her sciatica. He assumed his listening face; being a bone man, his knowledge of that illness was rudimentary, but he nodded and looked sympathetic while he wondered once again if Diana had exaggerated and why Emma hadn't told him her side of the story.

He glanced down the table once more and squashed a desire to get out of his chair, pick her up out of hers and carry her off home. The trouble was that they didn't see enough of each other.

CHAPTER EIGHT

'A VERY pleasant evening,' observed Sir Paul as they drove home.

'Delightful,' agreed Emma. It was fortunate that it was a short journey for there didn't seem to be anything else to say, and once they were at home she bade him a quiet goodnight and took herself off to bed. As she went up the stairs she hoped against hope that he would leap after her, beg her forgiveness... Of course he did no such thing!

In the morning when she went downstairs she found him on the point of leaving. 'I'll have to rearrange my day,' he told her. 'There's a patient—an emergency— for Theatre, so the list will run late. I'll probably be home around six o'clock, perhaps later. Don't forget that we are going to Mother's for the weekend.'

'Shall I take the dogs out?'

He was already through the door. 'I walked them earlier.' He nodded a goodbye and drove away as Mrs Parfitt came out of the kitchen.

'Sir Paul will knock himself out,' she observed, 'tearing off without a proper breakfast, up half the night working, and down here this morning before six o'clock, walking his legs off with those dogs.' She shook her head. 'I never did.'

Emma said, 'It's an emergency...'

'Maybe it is, but he didn't ought to go gallivanting

around before dawn after being up half the night—he's only flesh and blood like the rest of us.' She bent her gaze on Emma. 'Now you come and have your breakfast, ma'am; you look as though you could do with a bit of feeding up.'

When Emma got to the nursery she found Diana waiting for her.

'Emma, did Paul remember to tell you that I am giving a little party next week? Tuesday, I thought—it's one of his less busy days.'

She smiled, and Emma said, 'No, but we were out to dinner until late and he left early for the hospital.'

'Yes, I know,' said Diana, who didn't but somehow she made it sound like the truth. 'He works too hard; he'll overdo things if he's not careful. I'll try and persuade him to ease off a bit.'

'I think you can leave that to me, Diana. You know, you're so—so motherly you should find a husband,' Emma's smile was sweet. 'Well, I'll get started.'

She wished Maisie good morning and Maisie said, 'You're smouldering again. Been 'aving words?'

'I'm afraid so. I'm turning into a very unpleasant person, Maisie.'

'Not you—proper little lady, you are. Don't meet many of 'em these days. Now, that young woman downstairs...' She branched off into an account of the goings-on of the young couple on the landing below her flat and Emma forgot her seething rage and laughed a little.

'Doing anything nice this weekend?' asked Maisie as they sat feeding the babies.

'We're going to spend it with my husband's parents.'

'Like that, will you?'

'Oh, yes, they're such dears, and it's a nice old house

with a large garden. What are you going to do, Maisie? It's your weekend off, isn't it?'

'S'right.' Maisie looked coy. 'I got a bloke—'e's the milkman; we get on proper nice. Been courting me for a bit, 'e 'as, and we're thinking of having a go...'

'Oh, Maisie, how lovely. You're going to marry him?'

'I ain't said yes, mind you, but it'll be nice not ter 'ave ter come 'ere day in day out, with Madam looking down her nose at me.'

'You'll be able to stay home—oh, Maisie, I am glad; you must say yes. Does he got on well with your family?'

'They get on a treat. Yer don't think I'm silly?'

'Silly? To marry a man who wants you, who'll give you a home and learn to be a father to the children. Of course it's not silly. It's the nicest thing I've heard for days.'

'Oh, well, p'raps I will. Yer're 'appy, ain't yer?'

Emma was bending over Charlie's cot, tucking him in. 'Yes, Maisie.'

'Me, I'd be scared to be married to Sir Paul, that I would—never know what 'e's thinking. 'E don't show 'is feelings, do 'e?'

'Perhaps not, but they are there all the same.'

'Well, you should know,' said Maisie, and chuckled.

The weather was still bad later on, so Emma walked the dogs briefly and went home to sit by the fire. She had a lot to think about; Diana seemed very confident that Paul was in love with her and he had said nothing to give the lie to that, and there was that one remark that she would never forget—that she was worth twelve of Emma. 'Oh, well,' she told the dogs, 'we'll go to this party and see what happens.'

*   *   *

She was glad that they were going away for the weekend, for two days spent alone with Paul, keeping up a
façade of friendliness, was rather more than she felt she
could cope with. She packed a pretty dress, got into her
skirt and one of her cashmere jumpers, made up her face
carefully and declared herself ready to go directly after
breakfast on Saturday.

It was easier in the car, for she could admire the scen-
ery and there was no need to talk even though she longed
to. She sat watching his hands on the wheel—large, capable hands, well-kept. She loved them; she loved the
rest of him too and she wasn't going to sit back tamely
and let Diana dazzle him…

His parents welcomed them warmly, sweeping them
indoors while the dogs went racing off into the garden.
'And where is Queenie?' asked Mrs Wyatt.

'She's happy with Mrs Parfitt and they're company
for each other.'

'Of course. You're quite well again after that cold?
We missed seeing you while Paul was away. Such a
shame. Never mind, we'll make the most of you while
you are here. Let Paul take your coat, my dear, and come
and sit down and have some coffee.'

It was Mrs Wyatt who asked her how she had come
to catch cold. 'Paul tells me that you work twice a week
in a nursery in Moretonhampstead; I dare say you caught
it there.'

Emma didn't look at Paul. She murmured something
and waited to see if he would tell them how she had
caught a cold. He remained silent. As well he might, she
reflected crossly as he stood there looking faintly
amused. Really, he was a most tiresome man; if she
hadn't loved him so much she would have disliked him
intensely.

There might have been an awkward pause if he hadn't, with the ease of good manners, made some trifling remark about the weather. Smooth, thought Emma, and went pink when her mother-in-law said, 'Well, cold or no cold, I must say that marriage suits you, my dear.'

Emma put her coffee-cup down with care and wished that she didn't blush so easily. Blushing, she felt sure, had gone out with the coming of women's lib and feminism, whatever that was exactly. Mrs Wyatt, being of an older generation, wasn't concerned with either and found the blush entirely suitable.

Paul found it enchanting.

The weekend passed too quickly.

No one would ever replace her mother, but Mrs Wyatt helped to fill the emptiness her mother had left, and if she noticed the careful way Emma and Paul avoided any of the usual ways of the newly wed she said nothing.

Paul had never worn his heart on his sleeve but his feelings ran deep and, unless her maternal instinct was at fault, he was deeply in love with Emma. And Emma with him, she was sure of that. They had probably had one of the many little tiffs they would have before they settled down, she decided.

'You must come again soon,' she begged them as they took their leave on Sunday evening.

It was late by the time they reached the cottage, which gave Emma the excuse to go to bed at once. Paul's 'Goodnight, my dear,' was uttered in a placid voice, and he added that there was no need for her to get up for breakfast if she didn't feel like it. 'I shall be away all day,' he said. 'I've several private patients to see after I've finished at the hospital.'

In bed, sitting against the pillows with her knees under

her chin, Emma told Queenie, 'This can't go on, you know; something must be done.'

The Fates had come to the same conclusion, it seemed, for as Paul opened the front door the next evening, Emma, coming down the stairs, tripped and fell. He picked her up within seconds, scooping her into his arms, holding her close.

'Emma—are you hurt? Stay still a moment while I look.'

She would have stayed still forever with his arms around her, but she managed a rather shaky, 'I'm fine, really...'

He spoke to the top of her head, which was buried in his waistcoat. 'Emma—you must tell me—this ridiculous business of spending the night at that camp. Why did you refuse to listen to Diana? She is still upset and I cannot understand...'

Emma wrenched herself free. 'You listened to her and you believed her without even asking me. Well, go on believing her; you've known her for years, haven't you? And you've only known me for months; you don't know much about me, do you? But I expect you know Diana very well indeed.'

Paul put his hands in his pockets. 'Yes. Go on, Emma.'

'Well, if I were you, I'd believe her and not me,' she added bitterly. 'After all, she's worth a dozen of me.'

She flew back upstairs and shut her bedroom door with a snap and when Mrs Parfitt came presently to see if she should serve dinner she found Emma lying on her bed.

'I have such a shocking headache,' sighed Emma.

'Would you give Sir Paul his dinner? I couldn't eat anything.'

Indeed she did look poorly. Mrs Parfitt tut-tutted and offered one of her herbal teas. 'You just get into bed, ma'am. I'll tell Sir Paul and I dare say he'll be up to see you.'

'No, no, there's no need. Let him have his dinner first; he's had a busy day and he needs a meal and time to rest. I dare say it will get better in an hour or two.'

The headache had been an excuse, but soon it was real. Emma got herself into bed and eventually fell asleep.

That was how Paul found her when he came to see her. She was curled up, her tear-stained face cushioned on a hand, the other arm round Queenie. He stood studying her for some minutes. Her hair was loose, spread over the pillows, and her mouth was slightly open. Her cheeks were rather blotchy because of the tears but the long, curling brown lashes swept them gently. When he had fallen in love with her he hadn't considered her to be beautiful but now he could see that her ordinary little face held a beauty which had nothing to do with good looks.

He went away presently, reassured Mrs Parfitt and went to his study. There was always work.

Emma went down to breakfast in the morning, exchanged good mornings with Paul, assured him that her headache had quite gone and volunteered the information that she was going to the nursery that morning. 'And I said I would go tomorrow morning as well—they're short-handed for a few days. Will you be home late?'

'No, in time for tea I hope. There's the parish council meeting at eight o'clock this evening.'

'Oh, yes. I am helping with the coffee and biscuits.'

He left then, and very soon after she got into the Mini and drove herself to the nursery.

''Ere,' said Maisie as she sat down and picked up the first baby, 'wot yer been up ter? 'Ad a tiff?'

'No, no, Maisie. I'm fine, really. How's your intended?'

It was a red herring which took them through most of the morning.

It was just as Emma was leaving and passing the office that Diana called to her. 'Emma, don't worry if Paul is late this evening—he's coming to check one of the babies from the camp—a fractured arm as well as whooping cough.'

Emma asked, 'Did he say he'd come? He's got a parish meeting this evening; he won't want to miss it.'

Diana smiled slowly. 'Oh, I'm sure it won't matter if he's not there.' She stared at Emma. 'As a matter of fact, he said he was coming to see me anyway.'

'That's all right, then,' said Emma. She didn't believe Diana.

She had lunch, then took the dogs for a long walk and helped Mrs Parfitt get the tea. Buttered muffins and cucumber sandwiches, she decided, and one of Mrs Parfitt's rich fruit cakes.

Teatime came and went, and there was no Paul. At last she had a cup of tea anyway, and a slice of cake, helped Mrs Parfitt clear away and went upstairs to get ready. She put on a plain jersey dress suitable for a parish council meeting.

When seven o'clock came and went she told Mrs Parfitt to delay her cooking. 'Sir Paul won't have time to eat in comfort before eight o'clock. Perhaps we could have a meal when we get home?'

'No problem,' said Mrs Parfitt. 'The ragout'll only need warming up and the rest will be ready by the time you've had a drink.'

'You have your supper when you like, Mrs Parfitt.' Emma glanced at the clock; she would have to go to the meeting and make Paul's excuses.

The councillors were friendly and very nice about it. Doctors were never free to choose their comings and goings, observed old Major Pike, but he for one was delighted to see his little wife.

Emma smiled shyly at him—he was a dear old man, very knowledgeable about the moor, born and bred in Lustleigh even though he had spent years away from it. He thoroughly approved of her, for she was a local girl and looked sensible.

The meeting was drawing to a close when the door opened and Paul came in. Emma, sitting quietly at the back of the village hall, watched him as he made his excuses, exchanged a few laughing remarks with the rest of the council and sat down at the table. He hadn't looked at her, but presently he turned his head and gave her a look which shook her.

He was pale and without expression, and she knew that he was very angry. With her? she wondered. Had Diana been making more mischief between them? She hoped he would smile but he turned away and soon it was time for her to go and help the vicar's wife in the kitchen.

They made the coffee and arranged Petit Beurre biscuits on a plate and carried them through just as the chairman closed the meeting. Eventually goodnights were exchanged and everyone started to go home.

Emma, collecting cups and saucers, saw that Paul had stayed. Waiting for her, she supposed, and when she came from the kitchen presently he was still there.

He got up when he saw her, passed a pleasant time of day with the vicar's wife, helped them on with their coats, turned out the lights, locked the door and gave the key to the vicar, who had walked back for his wife. That done, he turned for home, his hand under Emma's elbow.

She sensed that it was an angry hand and, anxious not to make things worse than they apparently were, she trotted briskly beside him, keeping up with his strides.

In the drawing-room she sat down in her usual chair, but Paul stood by the door, the dogs beside him. Perhaps it would be best to carry the war into the enemy camp, Emma decided.

'You were very late; did you have an emergency?'

'No.'

'You went to see Diana...?'

'Indeed I did.'

Emma nodded. 'She told me that you would go and see her, and that you were going to see her anyway.'

'And you believed her?'

'Well, no, I didn't—but I do now.'

He said softly, 'And why do you suppose that I went to see her?'

Emma said carefully, 'Shall we not talk about that? Something has made you angry and you must be tired. I'll tell Mrs Parfitt that we are ready for dinner, shall I? While you have a drink.'

She was surprised when he laughed.

It was while they were eating that Paul said quietly, 'I do not wish you to go to the clinic any more, Emma.'

She had a forkful of ragout halfway to her mouth. 'Not go? Why ever not?'

'Would it do if I just asked you to do as I wish? There are good reasons.'

Emma allowed her imagination to run riot. Diana would have convinced him in her charming way that she was no good at the nursery, that she was too slow, too independent too. She said slowly, 'Very well, Paul, but I should like to go tomorrow morning to say goodbye to Maisie. I have been working with her and she is getting married—I've a present for her. And I'd like to see Charlie—he's so cross and unloved...'

'Of course you must go. Diana won't be there, but you could leave a note.'

'Very well. I'll think up a good excuse.'

She wrote it later when Paul was in his study. Obviously Paul didn't want her to meet Diana again. Why? she wondered. Perhaps she would never know. It had been silly of her to refuse to talk about it; she hadn't given him a chance to explain why he was angry. She thought that he still was but he had got his rage under control; his manner was imperturbable.

He had looked, she reflected, as though he could have swept the extremely valuable decanter and glasses off the side-table. She sighed—everything had gone wrong. Their marriage had seemed such a splendid idea and she had been sure that it would be a success.

The mousy little woman who deputised for Diana was at the nursery the next day.

'Is Diana ill?' asked Emma, agog for information.

'No, Lady Wyatt. She felt she should have a few days off; she's been working hard just lately. You'll be sorry to have missed her. I hear you're leaving us.'

'Yes, I'm afraid so. I shall miss the babies. May I go and say goodbye to them and Maisie?'

'Of course. I'm sure Diana is grateful for your help while you were with us.'

'I enjoyed it,' said Emma.

Maisie was on her own, and Emma resisted the urge to put on her pinny and give her a hand. 'I'm leaving, Maisie. I didn't want to but Sir Paul asked me to.'

'Did 'e now?' Maisie looked smug. She had been there yesterday evening when Sir Paul had come to see Diana and, although she hadn't been able to hear what was said, she had heard Diana's voice, shrill and then tearful, and Sir Paul's measured rumble. He had come out of the office eventually, and this time Maisie had been brave and stopped him before he got into his car.

'I don't know the ins and outs,' she had told him briskly, 'but it's time you caught on ter that Diana telling great whoppers about that little wife of yours. Little angel, she is, and never said a word, I'll bet. 'Oo pretended there weren't no doctors nor ambulances to go ter the camp? Moonshine. I 'eard 'er with me own ears telling 'em there weren't no need to send anyone. Sent little Emma back into all that mist and dark, she did, and tells everyone she'd done it awf her own bat and against 'er wishes.' Maisie had stuck her chin out. 'Sack me if yer want to. I likes ter see justice done, mister!'

Sir Paul had put out a hand and engulfed hers. 'Maisie—so do I. Thank you for telling me; Emma has a loyal friend in you.'

'Don't you go telling her, now.'

He had kept his word. Emma obviously knew nothing about his visit. Now everything would be all right. 'I'll miss yer, but I dare say you'll 'ave a few of yer own soon enough.'

Emma had picked up Charlie. 'I do hope Charlie will be wanted by someone.'

'Now, as ter that, I've a bit of good news. 'E's ter be adopted by such a nice woman and 'er 'usband—no kids of their own and they want a boy. 'E'll 'ave a good 'ome.'

'Oh, lovely. Maisie, will you write and tell me when you're to be married? And here's a wedding-present.'

Emma dived into her shoulder-bag and handed over a beribboned box.

'Cor, love, yer didn't orter…'

Maisie was already untying the ribbons. Inside was a brown leather handbag and, under that, a pair of matching gloves.

'I'll wear 'em on me wedding-day,' said Maisie, and got up and offered a hand.

Emma took it and then kissed Maisie's cheek. 'I hope you'll be very happy, and please write to me sometimes.'

'I ain't much 'and with a pen, but I'll do me best,' said Maisie.

Back home again, Emma took the dogs for a walk, had her lunch and then went into the garden. She pottered about, weeding here and there, tying things up, examining the rose bushes, anxious to keep busy so that she didn't need to think too much. She supposed that sooner or later she and Paul would have to talk—perhaps it would be best to get it over with. He had said that he would be home for tea. She began to rehearse a casual conversation—anything to prevent them talking about Diana.

The rehearsal wasn't necessary; when Paul got home he treated her with a casual friendliness which quite disarmed her. It was only later that she remembered she had told him that she had no wish to discuss the unfor-

tunate episode at the camp and Diana's accusations.
Which, of course, made it impossible for her to mention
it now. They spent the evening together, making trivial
talk, so that by the time she went to bed she was feeling
peevish from her efforts to think up something harmless
to say.

Paul got up to open the door for her, and as she went
past him with a quick goodnight he observed, 'Difficult,
isn't it, Emma?'

She paused to look up at him in surprise.

'Making polite small talk when you're bursting to utter quite different thoughts out loud.' He smiled down
at her—a small, mocking smile with a tender edge to it,
but she didn't see the tenderness, only the mockery.

For want of anything better, she said, 'I've no idea
what you mean.'

Over the next few days they settled down to an uneasy
truce—at least, it was uneasy on Emma's part, although
Paul behaved as though nothing had occurred to disturb
the easy-going relationship between them.

He was due up in Edinburgh at the beginning of the
following week, but he didn't suggest that she should go
with him. Not that I would have gone, reflected Emma,
all the same annoyed that he hadn't asked her.

He would be back in three days he told her. 'Why not
call Father to take you up to the Cotswolds, and spend
a couple of days with them?'

'Well, Mrs Parfitt did say that she would like a few
days to visit her sister at Brixham. I thought I might
drive her there and fetch her back. Willy and Kate can
sit in the back and I can leave Queenie for most of the
day.'

'You would like to do that? Then by all means go. I

don't really like your being alone in the house, though, Emma.'

'It won't be the first time, and I have the dogs. I'm not nervous.'

'I'll leave my phone number, of course. Perhaps it would be better if Mrs Parfitt waited until I am back home.'

'No, it wouldn't. There's lots more to do around the house and more cooking when you're home.'

'A nuisance in my own house, Emma?' He sounded amused.

'No—oh, no, of course not. But I know she'd prefer to go away when you're not here.'

'As you wish. In any case, I shall phone each evening.'

Paul left soon after breakfast, so Emma was able to drive Mrs Parfitt to her sister's very shortly after that.

It was a pleasant drive and the morning was fine, and when she reached Brixham she delivered Mrs Parfitt and then drove down to the harbour, where she parked the car and took the dogs for a run. She had coffee in a small café near by and then drove back to Lustleigh. When she reached the cottage and let herself in she realised that she felt lonely, despite the animals' company.

She wandered through the house, picking things up and putting them down again and, since Mrs Parfitt had left everything in apple-pie order, there was nothing for her to do except get the lunch.

A long walk did much to dispel her gloom and took up the time nicely until she could get her tea, and then it was the evening and Paul had said that he would phone...

She wondered how long it would take him to get

there; it was a long way and he might be too tired to ring up.

Of course he did, though; she was watching the six o'clock news when the phone rang and she rushed to it, fearful that he might ring off before she reached it.

Yes, his cool voice assured her, he had had a very pleasant drive, not all that tiring, and he had already seen two patients who needed his particular skills. 'I have a clinic tomorrow morning,' he told her, 'and then a lecture before dining with friends. I may phone rather later. You enjoyed your drive to Brixham?'

'Yes. We went for a long walk this afternoon; Willy got a thorn in his paw but I got it out. I'm getting their suppers…'

'In that case, don't let me keep you. Sleep well, Emma.'

He didn't wait for her answer but hung up.

An unsatisfactory conversation, thought Emma, snivelling into the dog food. He hadn't asked her if she was lonely or cautioned her kindly about locking up securely; indeed, he had asked hardly any questions about her at all.

She poked around in the fridge and ate two cold sausages and a carton of yoghurt, then took herself off to bed after letting the dogs out and then bolting and barring all the doors and the windows. She had no reason to feel nervous—it was a pity that she didn't know that the village constable, alerted by Sir Paul, had made it his business to keep an eye on her.

She lay awake for a long time, thinking about Paul. She missed him dreadfully; it was as though only half of her were alive—to have him home was all she wanted, and never mind if they no longer enjoyed their pleasant comradeship. She would have to learn to take second place to Diana and be thankful for that.

'But why he couldn't have married her and been done with it, I don't know,' Emma observed to the sleeping Queenie and, naturally enough, got no answer.

She walked to the village stores after breakfast, took her purchases home and went off for another walk with the dogs. The fine weather held and the sun shone, and out on the moors her worries seemed of no account. They went back home with splendid appetites and, having filled the dogs' bowls and attended to Queenie's more modest needs, Emma had her own lunch. The day was half done, and in the evening Paul would phone again.

She was putting away the last spoons and forks when there was a thump on the door-knocker. She wiped her hands on her apron and went to open it.

Diana stood there, beautifully dressed, exquisitely made-up, and smiling.

'Emma—I've been lunching at Bovey Tracey and I just had to come and see you. I know Paul's in Edinburgh and I thought you might like a visit. I'm surprised he didn't take you with him. It's great for a professor's image to have a wife, you know.'

She had walked past Emma as she held the door open and now stood in the hall, looking round. 'Nothing's changed,' she observed and heaved a sigh. 'I never liked that portrait over the table, but Paul said he was a famous surgeon in his day and he wouldn't move him.'

She smiled at Emma, and Emma smiled back. 'Well, it is Paul's house,' she said pleasantly. 'Would you like a cup of coffee?'

'I'd love one.' Diana had taken off her jacket and

thrown it over a chair. 'I had the most ghastly lunch at the Prostle-Hammetts and the coffee was undrinkable.'

It was the kind of remark Diana would make, thought Emma as she led the way into the drawing-room.

'Oh, the dogs,' cried Diana. 'We always had such fun together...'

Neither dog took any notice of her, which cheered Emma enormously—they were on her side.

'Do sit down,' she said. 'I'll fetch the coffee.'

'Can I help? I know my way around, you know.'

'No, no. Sit down here—you look a bit pinched. I expect you're tired.' She saw Diana's frown and the quick peek in the great Chippendale mirror over the fireplace.

In the kitchen she poured the coffee and wondered why Diana had come. To see how she had settled in as Paul's wife? Or just to needle her? Emma told herself stoutly that she wasn't going to believe anything Diana said. After all, so far she had done nothing but hint at her close friendship with Paul; all that nonsense about her love distracting him from his work had been nothing but moonshine. All the same, Diana had played a dirty trick on her when she had been at the nursery and she wasn't to be trusted.

She took the coffee-tray in, offered sugar and cream and sat down opposite her unwelcome guest. She didn't believe that Diana had called out of friendliness—it was probably just out of curiosity.

'Paul has a busy few days in Edinburgh,' said Diana. 'Patients yesterday and today after that long drive, and a clinic tomorrow. What a blessing it is that he has good friends—we always dined there...' She cast a sidelong look at Emma and gave a little laugh. 'Of course, everyone expected us to marry.'

'Then why didn't you?' Emma lifted the coffee-pot. 'More coffee?'

'No, thanks—I have to think of my figure.'

Emma said pertly, 'Well, yes, I suppose you do; we none of us grow any younger do we?'

Diana put her cup and saucer down. 'Look, Emma, you don't like me and I don't like you, but that doesn't alter the fact that Paul still loves me. He married you for all kinds of worthy reasons: you're an ideal wife for a busy man who is seldom at home; you don't complain; you're not pretty enough to attract other men. I dare say you're a good housewife and you won't pester him to take you out to enjoy the bright lights. As I said, you're an ideal wife for him. He's fond of you, I suppose—but loving you? I don't suppose you know what that means; you're content with a mild affection, aren't you? Whereas he...'

She had contrived to get tears in her eyes and Emma, seeing them, had sudden doubts.

'We love each other,' said Diana quietly. 'He has married you and he'll be a kind and good husband to you but you must understand that that is all he will ever be. I know you think I'm not worthy of him, and I know I'm not.' She blinked away another tear. 'He's not happy, you know, Emma.'

Emma said, 'You could go away—right away.'

Diana said simply, 'He would come after me—don't you know that? There's nothing I can do—I've talked and talked and he won't listen.' She looked at Emma. 'It is you who must go, Emma.'

Emma, looking at her and not trusting her an inch, found herself half believing her. She detested Diana, but if Paul loved her that didn't matter, did it? However, she didn't quite believe Diana; she would need proof.

Where would she get proof? It would have to be something that would hold water, not vague hints. She said, 'I don't intend to go, Diana.'

She got up to answer the phone and it was Paul. His quiet voice sounded reassuring to her ear. 'It will be late before I can phone you this evening so it seemed sensible to do so now. Is everything all right at home?'

'Yes, thank you—have you been busy?'

'Yes. I'll be here for another two days. Do you fetch Mrs Parfitt back tomorrow?'

'No, the day after.'

'You're not lonely?'

'No. Diana is here, paying a flying visit.'

She heard the change in his voice. 'I'll speak to her, Emma.'

'It's Paul; he'd like a word with you.' Emma handed the phone to Diana. 'I'll take the coffee out to the kitchen.'

Which she did, but not before she heard Diana's rather loud, 'Darling...'

CHAPTER NINE

EMMA hesitated for a moment; to nip back and listen at the door was tempting, but not very practical with the coffee-tray in her hands. She went to the kitchen, letting the door bang behind her, put the tray on the table and then returned noiselessly to the hall. The drawing-room door was ajar; she could hear Diana very clearly.

'I'll be at home until Friday. Goodbye, Paul.'

Emma retreated smartly to the kitchen and rattled a few cups and saucers and then went back to the drawing-room, shutting the baize door to the kitchen with a thump. Diana was putting on her coat.

'My dear, I must go. Thanks for the coffee, and I'm so glad to see that you've altered nothing in the cottage.' She paused, pulling on her gloves. 'Emma, you will think over what I have said, won't you? It sounds cruel but we are all unhappy now, aren't we? If you let Paul go then there would be only one of us unhappy, and since you don't love him you'll get over it quickly enough. He'll treat you well—financially, I mean.'

'I think you'd better go,' said Emma, 'before I throw something at you.' She went ahead of Diana and opened the cottage door. 'You're very vulgar, aren't you?'

She shut the door before Diana could reply.

She went back to the drawing-room and sat down; Queenie got on to her lap while Willy and Kate settled beside her. She didn't want to believe Diana but she had sounded sincere and she had cried. Moreover, she had told Paul that she would be at home until Friday. Why would she do that unless she expected him to go and see her? There was no way of finding out—at least, until Paul came home again.

He phoned the following evening. 'You're all right?' he wanted to know. 'Not lonely?'

'Not in the least,' said Emma airily. 'I had tea with the Postle-Hammets. I like Mrs Postle-Hammet and the children are sweet; I enjoyed myself.'

Largely because Mrs Postle-Hammet had been remarkably frank about her opinion of Diana, she thought. 'Cold as a fish and selfish to the bone and clever enough to hide it,' she had said—hardly information she could pass on to Paul.

'I should be home tomorrow evening, but if I should be delayed will you leave the side-door locked but not bolted? You'll fetch Mrs Parfitt tomorrow?'

'Yes, after lunch.'

'Good. I'll say goodnight, Emma. I've several more phone calls to make.' One of them to Diana? she wondered, and tried not to think about that.

She had an early lunch the next day and drove to Brixham through driving rain to fetch Mrs Parfitt, and then drove home again, listening to that lady's account of her few days' holiday. 'Very nice it was too, ma'am, but my sister isn't a good cook and I missed my kitchen. Still, the sea air was nice and there are some good shops. You've not been too alone, I hope?'

'No, no, Mrs Parfitt. I've been out to tea and Miss Pearson came to see me and Sir Paul has phoned each evening, and of course there were the dogs to take out. I had no time to be lonely—' Emma turned to smile at her companion '—but it's very nice to have you back, Mrs Parfitt. The cottage doesn't seem the same without you. Sir Paul is coming back this evening.'

'He'll need his dinner if he's driving all that way. Did you have anything in mind, ma'am?'

They spent the rest of the journey deciding on a menu to tempt him when he got home. 'Something that won't spoil,' cautioned Emma, 'for I've no idea exactly when he'll be back.'

Mrs Parfitt took off her best hat and her sensible coat and went straight to the kitchen. 'A nice cup of tea,' she observed, 'and while the kettle's boiling I'll pop a few scones in the oven.'

Emma went from room to room, making sure that everything was just so, shaking up cushions, rearranging the flowers, laying the pile of letters on the table by Paul's chair and, since it was going to be a gloomy evening, switching on lamps here and there so that there was a cheerful glow from the windows.

Satisfied that everything was as welcoming as she could make it, she went upstairs and changed into a patterned silk jersey dress, did her face with care and brushed her hair into a knot at the back of her head; it took a long time to get it just so but she was pleased with the result. Then she went downstairs to wait.

At ten o'clock she sent Mrs Parfitt to bed and ate a sketchy meal off a tray in the kitchen. When the long case clock in the hall chimed one o'clock she went to bed herself.

She was still awake when it chimed again, followed by the silvery tinkle of the carriage clock in the drawing-room. She slept after that but woke when it was barely light to creep downstairs to see if Paul was home. If he was, the back door would be bolted. It wasn't!

Emma stared at it for a long moment and then went to the phone and picked it up. The night porter answered it. Yes, Sir Paul had been in the hospital during the late evening and had left again shortly after—he had seen him leave in his car.

He sounded a little surprised at her query and she hastened to say that it was perfectly all right. 'Sir Paul said that he might do that. I'll ring him now. Thank you.'

She went to the kitchen then, and put on the kettle. She spooned tea into the pot, trying not to think about the previous evening, trying not to believe Diana's remarks but quite unable to forget them.

She was making tea when the kitchen door opened and Paul walked in. Emma caught her breath and choked on a surge of strong feelings.

'A fine time to come home,' she snapped, rage for the moment overcoming the delight of seeing him again, and she made unnecessary work of refilling the kettle and putting it back on the Aga.

Sir Paul didn't speak, but stood in the doorway looking at her indignant back, and since the silence was rather long she asked stiffly, 'Would you like a cup of tea?'

'Er—no, thank you, Emma. I'm sorry if you were worried.'

'Worried? Why should I be worried?' said Emma at her haughtiest. 'I phoned the hospital early this morning and I was told that you had been in and gone again late last night.' She drew a long breath. 'So I had no need to worry, had I?'

When he most annoyingly didn't answer, she said, 'I knew where you were...'

'Indeed.'

She had her back to him, busy with mug and sugar

and milk and pouring tea. 'Well, Diana came to see me—I told you that—you spoke to her...'

'Ah, Diana—of course. *Latet anguis in herba*!' murmured Sir Paul.

Emma's knowledge of Latin was sketchy and, anyway, what had grass got to do with it? For she had recognised the word *herba*, and if he was trailing a red herring she meant to ignore it. In any case her tongue was running on now, regardless of prudence.

'So of course I knew you'd go to her when you got back. She was very—very frank.' She gave an angry snuffle. 'She was glad I hadn't altered the pictures or anything.' She wouldn't look at him. 'Would you like breakfast?'

'No, Emma, I'll shower and change and go to the hospital.'

'You'll be back later? Teatime?'

'Don't count on that.' He spoke quietly, and something in his voice made her turn to look at him. He looked very tired but he gave her a bland stare from cold eyes. She had no doubt that he was angry. She was angry too, and miserable, and she loved him so much that she felt the ache of it. The urge to tell him so was so great that she started to speak, but she had barely uttered his name when he went away.

He had left the house by the time she had dressed and gone back downstairs to find Mrs Parfitt in the kitchen.

'Gone again,' cried Mrs Parfitt. 'I saw him drive off not ten minutes ago. By the time I'd got downstairs he'd gone. He'll wear himself out, that he will. How about a nice leg of lamb for dinner this evening? He'll need his strength kept up.'

When Emma said that he had come home very early in the morning Mrs. Parfitt commented, 'Must have been an accident. Now you go and eat your breakfast, ma'am, for no doubt you've been worrying half the night. Who'd be a doctor's wife, eh?' She laughed, and Emma echoed it in a hollow way.

She took the dogs for their walk after breakfast while Mrs Parfitt took herself off to the village shop and paid a visit to the butcher. It was while she was drying the dogs in the outhouse by the kitchen that Mrs Parfitt joined her.

'Postie was in the stores—there's been a nasty accident on the M5 where it turns into the A38.' Mrs Parfitt paused for breath, bursting with her news. 'Nine cars, he said, all squashed together, and Sir Paul right behind them on his way back here. Goes back to the hospital and spends the night in the operating theatre, he does. He's back there now, no doubt, working himself to death. He didn't ought to do it. He didn't say nothing to you, ma'am? No—well, of course, he wouldn't; he'd have known how upset you'd have been.'

Emma had gone very pale. 'Not a word. He didn't want tea or his breakfast but he said he had to go back.' The full horror of what she had said to him dawned on her—she had accused him of being with Diana while all the time he had been saving lives. She hadn't even given him the chance to tell her anything. She felt sick at the thought, and Mrs Parfitt took her arm and sat her down by the table.

'There, I shouldn't have come out with it so quick; you're that pale—like a little ghost. You stay there while I fetch you a drop of brandy.'

Emma was only too willing to sit. It was chilly in the little room, and the dogs, released from the tiresome business of being cleaned up before going into the house, had slipped away to lie by the Aga.

Mrs Parfitt came back with the brandy. 'It don't do to give way, ma'am,' she urged Emma. 'He's safe and sound even if he's tired to his bones, but you must show a bright face when he gets home, for that'll be what he needs.'

Emma drank the brandy, although she thought he wouldn't care if her face was bright or not. He would be polite, because he had beautiful manners and they wouldn't allow him to be otherwise, but he would have gone behind the barrier she had always sensed was between them—only now that barrier was twice as high and she doubted if she would ever climb it.

She spent a restless day, dreading his return and yet longing for it, going over and over in her aching head the awful things she had said and rehearsing the humble speech she would offer him when he came home. Which he did just as Mrs Parfitt brought in the tea-tray, following her into the drawing-room.

'There,' said Mrs Parfitt. 'Didn't I bake that fruit cake knowing you'd be here for your tea? I'll fetch another cup and a sandwich or two.'

She trotted off; she firmly believed that the way to a man's heart was through his stomach, and his doubtless needed filling.

He thanked her quickly and stooped to fondle the dogs weaving around his feet. 'Hello, Emma,' he said quietly.

'Paul.' The strength of her feelings was choking her as she got out of her chair, spilling an indignant Queenie on to the carpet. She said stupidly, 'I didn't know...' Her tongue shrivelled under his cold stare; underneath his quietness he was furiously angry, and suddenly she was angry again. 'Why didn't you tell me?'

He sat down in his chair and the dogs curled up beside

him. 'I don't believe that I had the opportunity,' he observed mildly.

'You could have—' Emma burst out, only to be interrupted by Mrs Parfitt with fresh tea, cup and saucer and a plate of sandwiches.

'Gentleman's Relish,' she pointed out in a pleased voice. 'Just what you fancy, sir, and cucumber and cress. I shall be serving dinner a bit earlier, ma'am? I dare say the master's peckish.'

Emma glanced at Paul, who said, 'That would be very nice, Mrs Parfitt.' He sounded like any man just home and sitting by his own fireside but Emma, unwittingly catching his eye, blinked at its icy hardness.

After Mrs Parfitt had gone Emma poured the tea, offered sandwiches and strove to think of something to say; she would have to apologise, and she wanted to, but for the moment the right words eluded her. All the same she made a halting start, only to have it swept aside as Paul began a conversation which gave her no chance to utter a word.

It was an undemanding and impersonal stream of small talk, quiet and unhurried. He could have been soothing a scared patient before telling her his diagnosis. Well, she wasn't a patient but she was scared, and the diagnosis, when it came, left her without words.

She was pouring his second cup of tea when he said casually, 'I've been offered a lecture tour in the States...'

He watched her pale face go even paler and saw the shock in it.

'The States? America? For how long?'

'Four months.'

She gulped back a protesting scream. 'That's a long time.'

'Yes. Time enough for us to consider our future, don't you agree?'

If only he wasn't so pleasant about it, Emma thought unhappily, and if only I could think of the right thing to say. After a minute she said, 'I expect you'd like to go?'

He didn't answer that so she tried again, asking a question her tongue uttered before she could stop it. 'Will you go alone?'

'Oh, yes.'

He didn't add to that, and she seized the opportunity and plunged into a muddled apology. None of the things she had meant to say came out properly. 'I'm sorry, Paul, I'm so very sorry; it was terribly stupid of me and unkind…'

He stopped her quite gently. 'Don't say any more, Emma. I thought that when we married…' He paused. 'You must see that if you don't trust me our marriage is going to be unhappy. That is why I shall go on this tour; you will have time to decide what you want to do with your future.'

She gave him a bewildered look. 'You mean, you don't want me to be your wife?'

'I didn't say that…'

'Well, no—but I think you meant that, only you are too polite to say so. I expect it's a good idea.'

At the end of four months, she thought sadly, he would come back, and they would separate without fuss and he would go his way and she would go hers. What about Diana? He hadn't mentioned her, had he? And she didn't dare to ask.

'I've made you very angry.'

'Indeed you have,' he agreed politely.

'I think it would have been better if you had shouted at me…'

'I could never shout at you, Emma.'

He smiled a little, thinking that he wanted to pick her up and shake her and carry her off somewhere and never let her go—his darling Emma.

Perhaps he was too old for her; perhaps she regretted marrying him. Certainly she had been a constantly good companion, and at times he had thought that she might become more than that, but once she had got over the shock she had given no sign that she didn't want him to go away. Indeed, she had taken it for granted that she would stay here.

He got up. 'I've one or two letters to write,' he told her. 'I'll go and do them before dinner—I can take the dogs out later.'

Emma nodded, and when he had gone carried the tray out to the kitchen. She stayed there for ten minutes, getting in Mrs Parfitt's way, and presently went back to the drawing-room and got out her embroidery. She wasn't being very successful with it and spent the next half-hour unpicking the work she had done the previous evening. It left her thoughts free and she allowed them full rein.

Somehow she must find a way to convince Paul that she was truly sorry. If he wanted to be free—perhaps to marry Diana—then the least she could do was to make it easy for him. She owed him so much that she could never repay him. She must find out when this lecture tour was to start; if she were to go away first, then he wouldn't need to go.

Her head seethed with plans; she could tell everyone that an aunt or uncle needed her urgently. That she had no relations of any kind made no difference—no one was to know that. She would do it in a way that would arouse no suspicions. Diana would guess, of course—

she had suggested it in the first place—but she wasn't likely to tell anyone.

She would write a letter to Paul, saying all the things she wanted to say—that she loved him and wanted him to be happy and thanked him for his kindness and generosity. Her mind made up, she attacked her embroidery with vigour and a complete disregard for accuracy.

Out-patients' sister watched Sir Paul's vast back disappear down the corridor. 'Well, what's the matter with him?' she asked her staff nurse. 'I've never known him dash off without his cup of tea, and him so quiet too. Something on his mind, do you suppose? He's got that nice little wife to go home to and you're not telling me that they're not happy together. Mention her and his face lights up—looks ten years younger. Ah, well, he'll go home and spend a lovely evening with her, I dare say.'

Sir Paul drove himself to the nursery, got out of his car and walked into Diana's office. She was getting ready to go home but put her jacket down as he went in. 'Paul, how lovely to see you—it's ages.'

He closed the door behind him—a disappointment to Maisie, who was getting ready to go home too, standing in the cloakroom near enough to the office to hear anything interesting which might be said.

'Perhaps you will spare me ten minutes, Diana?'

He hadn't moved from the door and she sat down slowly. 'All the time in the world for you, Paul.'

'You went to see Emma—why?'

She shrugged her shoulders. 'I thought she might be lonely.'

'The truth, Diana…'

Now Maisie edged nearer the door. She couldn't hear what was being said but she could hear Diana's voice getting more and more agitated, and Sir Paul's voice sounding severe and, presently, angry.

Sir Paul wasn't mincing his words. 'I have never at any time given you reason to believe that I was in love with you.' He added, with brutal frankness, 'Indeed, you are the last woman I would wish to have for a wife.'

Maisie, her ear pressed to the keyhole, just had time to nip back into the cloakroom as he opened the door.

He saw at once on his return home that this was not the right time to talk to Emma. She was being carefully polite and the expression on her face warned him not to be other than that; so the evening was spent in a guarded manner, neither of them saying any of the things they wanted to say, both waiting for some sign...

Emma went to bed rather early, relieved that she was alone and could grizzle and mope and presently go over her plans to leave. Just for a little while that evening, despite their coolness towards each other, she had wondered if she could stay, if they could patch things up between them. But trying to read Paul's thoughts was an impossible task; they were far too well hidden behind his bland face. He wasn't going to reproach her; he wasn't going to say another word about the whole sorry business. Presumably it was to be forgotten and they would go on as before, just good friends and then, when the right moment came, parting.

'I hate Diana,' said Emma, and kicked a cushion across the floor. 'I hope she makes him very unhappy.' It was a palpable lie which did nothing to restore her spirits.

She didn't sleep much—she was too busy making plans. Many were wildly unsuitable to begin with, but by the early morning she had discarded most of them in favour of one which seemed to her to be simple and foolproof.

She would give Mrs Parfitt a day off—it would have to be in two days' time, when Paul had his theatre list and a ward round, which meant he wouldn't be home before about six o'clock. Once Mrs Parfitt was out of the house she would pack a few things in a suitable bag, write a letter to Paul and one to Mrs Parfitt—the illness of a fictitious aunt would do very well—walk to Bovey Tracey, get a bus down to the main road and another bus to Plymouth.

She could lose herself there and get a job in a restaurant or a hotel—surely there would be temporary jobs in the tourist trade. She would have to buy some kind of a bag—a knapsack would do. In the morning she would take her car into Exeter and get one. It was morning already, she reminded herself, and got up and dressed and did the best she could to disguise her sleepless night.

Sir Paul bade her good morning in his usual manner, remarked on the fine day and studied her tired face. She looked excited, too, in a secret kind of way, as though she were hatching some plot or other. He decided to come home early but told her smoothly when she asked if he would be home for tea that he thought it unlikely, watching the relief on her face.

It was easy to get Mrs Parfitt to take a day off; Emma knew that she wanted to go to Exeter and buy a new hat. 'Take the whole day,' she suggested. 'I might go over to Mrs Postle-Hammett's—it's a good walk for the dogs and she's very fond of them. I'm sure Sir Paul will give you a lift tomorrow morning.'

'Well, if you don't mind, ma'am. I must say I'd like a day to shop around.'

'I'm going to Exeter this morning,' said Emma. 'One

or two things I want. Do we need anything for the house while I'm there?'

There was nothing needed. She went to her room and got into her jacket, found her car keys and drove herself to Exeter. She soon found exactly what she wanted in a funny little shop at the bottom of the high street, walked back to the car park in Queen Street and on the way came face to face with Maisie.

'Come and have a cup of coffee?' said Emma. She was glad to see her and steered her into a café. 'Aren't you at the nursery any more?'

'Leaving on Saturday,' said Maisie and looked coy. 'Getting married, yer see.'

'On Saturday? Oh, Maisie, I am glad; I hope you'll both be very happy. In church?'

'Baptist. Just the kids and 'is mum and dad.' Masie sugared her coffee lavishly. 'Saw yer old man at the nursery—leastways, 'eard 'im. In a bit of a rage, it sounded like, and that Diana going 'ammer and tongs. Sounded all tearful she did—kept saying, "Oh, Paul, oh, Paul." Didn't come to work today neither. Nasty piece of work she is; turns on the charm like I switches on the electric.'

'She's very attractive,' said Emma, and felt sick. So, he was still seeing Diana; it was a good thing she had decided to go…

'Suppose so,' said Maisie. 'Leastways, to men. Good thing you're married to yer old man!'

She chuckled and Emma managed a laugh. 'Yes, isn't it? Tell me what you're going to wear…'

Which filled the next ten minutes very nicely before Maisie declared that she still had some shopping to do.

'We'll 'ave some photos,' she promised. 'I'll send you one.'

'Please do, Maisie, and it was lovely meeting you like that.'

They said goodbye and Emma went back to the car and drove home. The small hopeful doubt she had had about leaving had been doused by Maisie's news. Tomorrow she would go.

She was surprised when Paul came home at teatime, but she greeted him in what she hoped was a normal voice, and, when he asked her, told him that she had been to Exeter—'One or two things I wanted'—and had met Maisie. Maisie's approaching wedding made a good topic of conversation; Emma wore it threadbare and Paul, listening to her repeating herself, decided that whatever it was she was planning it wouldn't be that evening.

He went to his study presently and spent some time on the phone rearranging the next day's work. When his receptionist complained that he had several patients to see on the following afternoon he told her ruthlessly to change their appointments. 'I must have the whole of tomorrow afternoon and evening free,' he told her, and then spent ten minutes charming Theatre Sister into altering his list.

'I'll start at eight o'clock instead of nine,' he told her, and, since she liked him and admired him, she agreed, aware that it would mean a good deal of rearranging for her to do.

As for his registrar, who admired him too, he agreed cheerfully to take over out-patients once the ward-round was done.

Sir Paul ate his supper, well aware that he had done all he could to avert whatever disaster his Emma was plotting.

        *   *   *

The cottage seemed very empty once Paul and Mrs Parfitt had gone the next morning. It was still early; she had all day before her. Emma took the dogs for a long walk, went from room to room tidying up, clearing the breakfast things Mrs Parfitt hadn't had the time to do, and then she sat down to write her letters.

This took her a long time, for it was difficult to write exactly what she wanted to say to Paul. She finished at last, wrote a letter to Mrs Parfitt about the sick aunt and went to pack her knapsack. Only the necessities went into it—her lavish wardrobe she left. She left her lovely sapphire and diamond ring too, putting it in its little velvet box on the tallboy in his dressing-room.

She wasn't hungry but she forced herself to eat some lunch, for she wasn't sure where she would get her supper. She had some money too—not very much but enough to keep her for a week, and as soon as she had a job she would pay it back; she had been careful to put that in her letter.

It was going on for three o'clock by then. She got her jacket, changed into sensible shoes, took the dogs for a quick run and then carefully locked up the house. It only remained for her to take her letter and leave it in Paul's study.

She left the knapsack in the hall with Mrs Parfitt's letter and went to the study. The letter in her hand, she sat for a moment in his chair, imagining him sitting in it presently, reading her letter, and two tears trickled down her cheeks. She wiped them away, got out of the chair and went round the desk and leaned over to prop the letter against the inkstand.

Sir Paul's hand took it gently from her just as she set it down, and for a moment she didn't move. The sight of the sober grey sleeve, immaculate linen and gold cufflinks, and his large, well-kept hand appearing from no-where, had taken her breath, but after a moment she turned round to face him. 'Give it to me, please, Paul.' Her voice was a whisper.

'But it is addressed to me, Emma.'

'Yes, yes, I know it is. But you weren't to read it until after…'

'You had gone?' he added gently. 'But I am here, Emma, and I am going to read it.'

The door wasn't very far; she took a step towards it but he put out an arm and swept her close. 'Stay here where you belong,' he said gently and, with one arm holding her tight, he opened the letter.

He read it and then read it again, and Emma tried to wriggle free.

'Well, now you know,' she said in a watery voice. 'What are you going to do about it? I didn't mean to fall in love with you—it—it was an accident; I didn't know it would be so—so… What are you going to do, Paul?'

His other arm was round her now. 'Do? Something I wanted to do when I first saw you.' He bent and kissed her, taking his time about it.

Emma said shakily, 'You mustn't—we mustn't—what about Diana?'

'I can see that we shall have to have a cosy little talk, my darling, but not yet.' He kissed her again. 'I've al-ways loved you. You didn't know that, did you? I didn't tell you, for I hurried you into marriage and you weren't ready for me, were you? So I waited, like a fool, and somehow I didn't know what to do.'

'It was me,' said Emma fiercely into his shoulder. 'I listened to Diana and I don't know why I did. I suppose it was because I love you and I want you to be happy, and I thought it was her and not me.' She gave a great sniff. 'She's so beautiful and clever and the babies were darlings and she told me to go to the travellers' camp...'

Sir Paul, used to the occasional incoherence of his patients, sorted this out. 'Darling heart, you are beautiful and honest and brave, and the only woman I have ever loved or could love.' He gave a rumble of laughter. 'And you shall have a darling baby of your own...'

'Oh, I shall love that—we'll share him. Supposing he's a girl?'

'In that case we must hope that we will be given a second chance.'

His arms tightened round her and she looked up at him, smiling. 'We'll start all over again—being married, I mean.'

He kissed her once more. 'That idea had occurred to me too.'

EVER HAD ONE OF THOSE DAYS?

TO DO:

☑ at the supermarket buying two dozen muffins that your son just remembered to tell you he needed for the school treat, you realize you left your wallet at home

☑ at work just as you're going into the big meeting, you discover your son took your presentation to school, and you have his hand-drawn superhero comic book

☑ your mother-in-law calls to say she's coming for a month-long visit

☑ finally at the end of a long and exasperating day, you escape from it all with an entertaining, humorous and always romantic Love & Laughter book!

ENJOY
LOVE & LAUGHTER™
EVERY DAY!

For a preview, turn the page....

*Here's a sneak peek at
Carrie Alexander's THE AMOROUS HEIRESS
Available September 1997...*

———————

"YOU'RE A VERY popular lady," Jed Kelley observed as Augustina closed the door on her suitors.

She waved a hand. "Just two of a dozen." Technically true since her grandmother had put her on the open market. "You're not afraid of a little competition, are you?"

"Competition?" He looked puzzled. "I thought the position was mine."

Augustina shook her head, smiling coyly. "You didn't think Grandmother was the final arbiter of the decision, did you? I say a trial period is in order." No matter that Jed Kelley had miraculously passed Grandmother's muster, Augustina felt the need for a little propriety. But, on the other hand, she could be married before the summer was out and be free as a bird, with the added bonus of a husband it wouldn't be all that difficult to learn to love.

She got up the courage to reach for his hand, and then just like that, she—Miss Gussy Gutless Fairchild—was holding Jed Kelley's hand. He looked down at their linked hands. "Of course, you don't really know what sort of work I can do, do you?"

A funny way to put it, she thought absently, cradling his callused hand between both of her own. "We can

get to know each other, and then, if that works out..."
she murmured. *Wow.* If she'd known what this arranged
marriage thing was all about, she'd have been a sup-
porter of Grandmother's campaign from the start!

"Are you a palm reader?" Jed asked gruffly. His
voice was as raspy as sandpaper and it was rubbing her
all the right ways, but the question flustered her. She
dropped his hand.

"I'm sorry."

"No problem," he said, "as long as I'm hired."

"Hired!" she scoffed. "What a way of putting it!"

Jed folded his arms across his chest. "So we're back
to the trial period."

"Yes." Augustina frowned and her gaze dropped to
his work boots. Okay, so he wasn't as well off as the
majority of her suitors, but really, did he think she was
going to *pay* him to marry her?

"Fine, then." He flipped her a wave and, speechless,
she watched him leave. She was trembling all over like
a malaria victim in a snowstorm, shot with hot charges
and cold shivers until her brain was numb. This couldn't
be true. Fantasy men didn't happen to nice girls like her.

"Augustina?"

Her grandmother's voice intruded on Gussy's privacy.
"Ahh. There you are. I see you met the new gardener?"

Coming in August 1997!

THE BETTY NEELS
RUBY COLLECTION

August 1997—Stars Through the Mist
September 1997—The Doubtful Marriage
October 1997—The End of the Rainbow
November 1997—Three for a Wedding
December 1997—Roses for Christmas
January 1998—The Hasty Marriage

COLLECTOR'S EDITION

This August start assembling the
Betty Neels Ruby Collection. Six of the
most requested and best-loved titles have
been especially chosen for this collection.
From August 1997 until January 1998,
one title per month will be available to avid
fans. Spot the collection by the lush ruby red
cover with the gold Collector's Edition banner
and your favorite author's name—Betty Neels!

Available in August at your favorite retail outlet.

HARLEQUIN®

Take 4 bestselling love stories FREE

Plus get a FREE surprise gift!

Let's Celebrate!

LOVE & LAUGHTER™

invites you to
the party of the season!

Grab your popcorn and be prepared to laugh as we celebrate with **LOVE & LAUGHTER**.

Harlequin's newest series is going Hollywood!

Let us make you laugh with three months of terrific books, authors and romance, plus a chance to win a FREE 15-copy video collection of the best romantic comedies ever made.

For more details look in the back pages of any Love & Laughter title, from July to September, at your favorite retail outlet.

Don't forget the popcorn!

Available wherever
Harlequin books are sold.

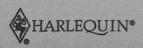

Look us up on-line at: http://www.romance.net

LLCELEB

If you are looking for more titles by

BETTY NEELS

Don't miss this chance to order more stories
by one of Harlequin's best-loved authors:

Harlequin Romance®

#03339	THE AWAKENED HEART	$2.99 U.S. $3.50 CAN.	☐ ☐
#03371	WEDDING BELLS FOR BEATRICE	$2.99 U.S. $3.50 CAN.	☐ ☐
#03389	A CHRISTMAS WISH	$2.99 U.S. $3.50 CAN.	☐ ☐
#03400	WAITING FOR DEBORAH	$3.25 U.S. $3.75 CAN.	☐ ☐

(limited quantities available on certain titles)

TOTAL AMOUNT	$	
POSTAGE & HANDLING	$	_____
($1.00 for one book, 50¢ for each additional)		
APPLICABLE TAXES*	$	
TOTAL PAYABLE	$	
(check or money order—please do not send cash)		

To order, complete this form and send it, along with a check or money order
for the total above, payable to Harlequin Books, to: **In the U.S.:** 3010 Walden
Avenue, P.O. Box 9047, Buffalo, NY 14269-9047; **In Canada:** P.O. Box 613,
Fort Erie, Ontario, L2A 5X3.

Name: _____

Address: _____ City: _____

State/Prov.: _____ Zip/Postal Code: _____

*New York residents remit applicable sales taxes.
 Canadian residents remit applicable GST and provincial taxes.   HBNBACK8

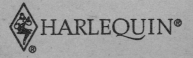

HARLEQUIN®

Look us up on-line at: http://www.romance.net

HARLEQUIN WOMEN KNOW ROMANCE WHEN THEY SEE IT.

And they'll see it on **ROMANCE CLASSICS**, the new 24-hour TV channel devoted to romantic movies and original programs like the special **Romantically Speaking-Harlequin® Goes Prime Time.**

Romantically Speaking-Harlequin® Goes Prime Time introduces you to many of your favorite romance authors in a program developed exclusively for Harlequin® readers.

Watch for **Romantically Speaking-Harlequin® Goes Prime Time** beginning in the summer of 1997.

If you're not receiving ROMANCE CLASSICS, call your local cable operator or satellite provider and ask for it today!

ROMANCE CLASSICS

Escape to the network of your dreams.

Free Gift Offer

As Seen on TV!

With a Free Gift proof-of-purchase
from any Harlequin® book, you can receive
a beautiful cubic zirconia pendant.

This stunning marquise-shaped stone is a genuine cubic
zirconia—accented by an 18" gold tone necklace.
(Approximate retail value $19.95)

Send for yours today...
compliments of ✦HARLEQUIN®

To receive your free gift, a cubic zirconia pendant, send us one original proof-of-purchase, photocopies not accepted, from the back of any Harlequin Romance®, Harlequin Presents®, Harlequin Temptation®, Harlequin Superromance®, Harlequin Intrigue®, Harlequin American Romance®, or Harlequin Historicals® title available at your favorite retail outlet, together with the Free Gift Certificate, plus a check or money order for $1.65 U.S./$2.15 CAN. (do not send cash) to cover postage and handling, payable to Harlequin Free Gift Offer. We will send you the specified gift. Allow 6 to 8 weeks for delivery. Offer good until December 31, 1997, or while quantities last. Offer valid in the U.S. and Canada only.

Free Gift Certificate

Name: _____

Address: _____

City: _____ State/Province: _____ Zip/Postal Code: _____

Mail this certificate, one proof-of-purchase and a check or money order for postage and handling to: HARLEQUIN FREE GIFT OFFER 1997. In the U.S.: 3010 Walden Avenue, P.O. Box 9071, Buffalo NY 14269-9057. In Canada: P.O. Box 604, Fort Erie, Ontario L2Z 5X3.